Waiting
for the
Queen

Also by Joanna Higgins

The Importance of High Places
A Soldier's Book
Dead Center

Waiting *for the* Queen

A Novel of Early America

Joanna Higgins

milkweed
editions

Although two characters in this book are historical personages—the Vicomte de Noailles and the Marquis Antoine Omer Talon—and other historical figures are alluded to, this is a work of fiction. The characters and events herein are either fictional or used fictitiously. Any similarity to real persons, living or dead, is unintended and coincidental except where substantiated by actual historical events.

Published 2013 by Milkweed Editions
Printed in Canada
Cover design by Rebecca Lown
Cover art by Elsa Mora
13 14 15 16 17   5 4 3 2 1
First Edition

Manufactured in Canada in July 2013 by Friesens Corporation.

Milkweed Editions, an independent nonprofit publisher, gratefully acknowledges sustaining support from the Bush Foundation; the Patrick and Aimee Butler Foundation; the Dougherty Family Foundation; the Driscoll Foundation; the Jerome Foundation; the Lindquist & Vennum Foundation; the McKnight Foundation; the voters of Minnesota through a Minnesota State Arts Board Operating Support grant, thanks to a legislative appropriation from the arts and cultural heritage fund, and a grant from the Wells Fargo Foundation Minnesota; the National Endowment for the Arts; the Target Foundation; and other generous contributions from foundations, corporations, and individuals. For a full listing of Milkweed Editions supporters, please visit www.milkweed.org.

Library of Congress Cataloging-in-Publication Data

Higgins, Joanna, 1945–
    Waiting for the queen / Joanna Higgins. — 1st ed.
        p.   cm.
    Summary: In 1793, fifteen-year-old Eugenie de la Roque, her family, and other nobles barely escape the French Revolution and arrive in Pennsylvania, where homesick young Hannah Kimbrell, a Shaker, is among those charged with preparing New France for the aristocrats' arrival.
    ISBN 978-1-57131-700-1 (alk. paper)
    [1. Frontier and pioneer life—Pennsylvania—Fiction. 2. Social classes—Fiction. 3. Friendship—Fiction. 4. Shakers—Fiction. 5. Slavery—Fiction. 6. Pennsylvania—History—1775–1865—Fiction. 7. France—History—Revolution, 1789–1799—Fiction.] I. Title.
    PZ7.H5349548Wai 2013
    [Fic]—dc23

                                                                                                                2012042167

Milkweed Editions is committed to ecological stewardship. We strive to align our book production practices with this principle, and to reduce the impact of our operations in the environment. We are a member of the Green Press Initiative, a nonprofit coalition of publishers, manufacturers, and authors working to protect the world's endangered forests and conserve natural resources. *Waiting for the Queen* was printed on acid-free 100% postconsumer-waste paper by Friesens Corporation.

To Kaili and Christopher

Waiting
for the
Queen

1793

Novembre / November

Eugenie ☙

A cold wind gusts through these American mountains, ruffling the churning river and further impeding the progress of our boats. On a map Papa showed us in Philadelphia, the river bears the Indian name Susquehanna as it meanders down through eastern Pennsylvania like gathered blue stitching on green fabric. The looping is most definitely accurate. But today the river is not blue; rather, nearly black. And the mountains are not green but in their sheer drapery of fog and mist, a dismal gray. Often a cask slides by, carried swiftly by the current. Or there might be great tree limbs with a few tufts of leaves that seem torn bits of flag. Our flag, I imagine in my fatigue. The flag of our beloved *la France*.

Cold penetrates wool and velvet and settles upon my shoulders like stones. Ah, the marquis's perfidy! Talon promised fine dwellings, but where are they? We have been traveling now for a week upon this wilderness river. He promised a French town, but where is it? I lean to my trembling pet and wrap my cloak more securely about her. "*Courage*, Sylvette. Soon we shall learn if the marquis is a man of honor or not."

Sylvette curls herself tightly against me, shivering in spasms. I try to comfort her, but a settlement appears along the bank that causes me to tremble as well—forest scraped clear for a few meters, and six rude log dwellings there, earthen colored. Smoke rises from chimneys, mingling with low cloud. Someone on a landing gestures toward our boats.

Mon Dieu! Can this be our promised town?

I close my eyes and hold onto Sylvette. When I open my eyes again, the settlement is behind us.

Merci, my Lady.

Fear eases its hold. I scratch behind Sylvette's ears, feel the warmth of her. She hides under her paw and dozes. By now it must be midafternoon. Early this morning we embarked from the usual sort of camp we've been seeing along this river, merely a few board houses surrounded by a cluster of squat log huts more like caves. Last evening and again early this morning, several ill-clothed women and children emerged from these dark dwellings to stare at us. Maman ignores the uncouth gaping Americans. I do as well. But when a child ran up to Papa, wanting to touch his fur-trimmed cloak, Papa leaned down and lifted the boy high into the air and swung him down again. The child ran off, but not far. *"Au revoir!"* Papa called. The urchin smiled and threw himself at Papa again, and again Papa swung him upward. This time the child reached for the feathers on Papa's high-crowned hat, but Papa set him down before he could tear them off. Then Papa took a coin from his waistcoat and gave it to him. Maman pretended to see nothing of this.

How these people bring to mind our peasants, the way they watch us. The boy's mother finally pulled him away as if we were evil.

For such reasons and many others, the journey north from the port of Philadelphia has been distressing—the first hundred or so miles in a bumping coach to the river town of Harrisburg, and now these low boats and rainswollen river. And along the way, poor inns, poor food, and poor sleep, I tossing about on thin mattresses stuffed with crackling straw, tormented by dreams that always leave me exhausted. And then the dreams' poisonous residue taints my days as well.

But the dipping boats lull, and it is difficult to keep my eyes open. I give in to temptation and am, at once, back at our château in the Rhône-et-Loire. The fields an orange sea, flames rising upon it like waves. I run down stone steps into a cellar. *Maman!* I call. *Papa!* But no sound issues from my throat. The cellar becomes a charred field, and I see a farm cart surrounded by peasants on the road bordering the field. In the cart, my beloved maid and companion, Annette. Then smoke rises from the cart. Spikes of flame. Peasants move back. The air around the cart brightens with fire.

I force my eyes open and the scene shrivels as if it, too, has burned.

"Ah, Sylvette." Her white fur warms my cheek, catches my tears.

Why, Papa, I remember asking, *did they do that to my Annette?*

Because of her royal blood.

Do they hate us so, then?

I think—yes.

But what have we done to them, Papa?

Perhaps it may not be what we have done, so much, but what we have failed to do.

And that is, Papa?

Treat them as we treat each other.

But, Papa, they are not like us, so how can we treat them that way?

Papa had no answer for me. He said only that the times are most confusing, and one is certain of little now.

My heart is beating so as I hold Sylvette. "Maman," I whisper, waking her. "How can there be fine dwellings in such a place? Perhaps they are taking us to some prison, just as they took the Queen to la Conciergerie!"

Maman shakes her head a little and stares at the river. Finally she whispers, "No, Eugenie. This is America. We have been promised refuge, remember?"

"But in such a wilderness? Why could we not have remained in Philadelphia? Philadelphia is America, too, is it not?"

"Eugenie, you well know why. Yellow fever has swept through there these past months, and now it is a city struggling against lawlessness and near anarchy. Did we flee the chaos and anarchy and terrible dangers in France only to endanger ourselves here? Of course not. Also, there are many Americans who favor the French rebels and would happily see us imprisoned or, worse, sent back to France—a death sentence for us! I wish to hear no more talk of returning to Philadelphia."

"But the Vicomte de Noailles was there, Maman."

"*Oui,* to arrange our passage and, earlier, to negotiate on our behalf. But you can be certain he will not remain. Even President George Washington has left for his home in Virginia. Far better for all of us to be some distance away, in a protected area, as Talon promises."

"*Promises,*" I cannot refrain from saying.

"And as for the yellow fever, I am thus reminded." She

takes two cloves of roasted garlic from her reticule, one for each of us.

"But Maman, the taste lingers, and my breath becomes foul. Besides, has there not been a frost? It is said that when the frosts come, the danger of fever is no—"

"Frost or not, eat it, Eugenie. The garlic cannot hurt, and it may help, still. Or would you rather douse your redingote and gown with vinegar as the slaves have been doing this week past?"

"And so have the slaves' master and his family. Well, what can it matter, those daughters being so long of face and foot. Gowns soused in vinegar will hardly make any difference for *them*."

Maman watches as I put the clove on my tongue. "You must swallow it now, Eugenie."

Reluctantly, I obey. "Those slaves, Maman. They endanger us as much as Philadelphia might. Are they not from the Caribbean, supposedly the source of the yellow fever? Why must they travel with us? It is beyond insulting. And remember how we heard they are from a rebellious area? What if their loyalty to Rouleau isn't so assured? How safe shall we be then? By allowing Rouleau and his slaves, the marquis has doubly betrayed us."

"Eugenie. We know not whether the marquis has betrayed us at all. And why should he not offer sanctuary to Rouleau? We cannot begrudge the man. He, too, has suffered. Besides, there are but four slaves and those, by all accounts, loyal. You have seen the scars on that one. It is said he tried to put out the fire in Rouleau's *maison*, a fire set by other slaves."

"Well, but Rouleau is not nobility, though he pretends

to be. A pompous little tyrant, ingratiating to us, but quite mean to his supposedly loyal slaves. No wonder the others rebelled, and perhaps these shall too. Maman, the Rouleau family cannot stay with us. Either they must go elsewhere or we must."

"Eugenie, we have no choice in this matter."

"But the stink of them! Dousing themselves in vinegar!"

"Lower your voice, please."

"Well, but we agree, do we not?"

"Your speech is too direct. It is not seemly."

"Yet it is the truth."

"The truth must be better clothed."

"Well, how can one better say that they are a threat to our lives? How can we best clothe that truth, Maman?"

"We could tell the marquis that we prefer not to have Caribbean slaves and commoners at the settlement. Better that they find more suitable accommodation elsewhere."

"But that hardly makes the point."

"It will express our displeasure."

"Surely we wish to express more than that."

Maman is silent.

"Well, I shall not douse Sylvette with vinegar. Nor my gowns."

"Of course not, my dear. Nor shall—"

Maman lurches against me as our longboat spins backward and into the prow of the boat behind us. Water sloshes in, wetting my suede shoes, redingote, and gown. Maman and I right ourselves, and there is the Rouleaux's youngest slave in the boat alongside us. Her cotton gown is sopping to the waist, her eyes wide with fright. The pole is useless in her hands.

II

"Idiots!" Rouleau shouts. I think he means us until he adds, "Look what you have done to the noble ladies and gentlemen! You shall be punished! Now, away from their boat!"

The younger of the male slaves pushes hard against his pole, his scarred face trembling with exertion. But the current is holding us locked fast, and both boats are losing hard-won distance.

"My fault, monsieur," Papa calls. "Do not punish them, I beg of you. I lost the bottom again. They are blameless."

"Nevertheless, comte, they should have steered clear in time."

I bow my head to hide tears. Papa, poling with slaves and savage-looking rivermen in deerskin jackets and fringed trousers stained black with tobacco juice. Papa making apology to Rouleau.

"Mademoiselle," Florentine du Vallier calls out. "Perhaps the lances on your family crest are in fact poles, do you think?" Florentine is sixteen and believes he is a great wit. He is also thin and pimply and, when not attempting jests, surly.

Still, the nobles in our boat laugh. Maman and I ignore them. But then elderly Duc d'Aversille, usually a kind and most generous man, addresses Papa, saying, "La Roque, had you remained in France, you might be wearing the revolutionists' red cap and tricolor cockade by now."

How dare he. I turn to stare at him and hope that Papa will come up with some sharp rejoinder, but Papa merely laughs along with everyone and then says, "If you knew what pleasure I derive from getting this boat to move in one direction or another, Duc, you would be vying for this work, I assure you."

"Not I, Philippe. I am far too old for such sport."

Everyone laughs again, but the Comtesse de Sevigy first gives us a falsely sympathetic look. Hypocrite! Supposedly, she is Maman's friend. Oh, I can just hear her. *Madame Queen, we have the most delightful little story to tell you about our river journey here. It seems that Comte de La Roque has kept his true talent hidden until now . . .*

It will ruin us.

But an even greater fear is that the events of these past months have overburdened Papa's mind.

The boats separate. Papa and the rivermen plant their poles in the river, lean forward, and pull. Our boat inches forward again. Rain drips from the rivermen's broad leather hats. It sluices down off the boat's canopy. Clouds descend even farther, obscuring the tops of these mountains bristling with leafless trees. But then Maman points to a patch of color on a mountainside—sienna, maroon, dark green, and lemon hues faded in the mist.

"*Chêne,*" Maman says. Oak. "And see that lighter shade? Lovely!"

"Like your brocade gown. Did you bring that one with you, Maman? You could wear it here, for the Queen. You know the one—you like to wear it on the Feast of All Saints Day." I stop, remembering how we observed that holy day quietly, in Philadelphia, with no pomp or feasting whatsoever. Maman had worn one of her other, simpler, gowns.

"*Non,*" she says. "I did not bring it." After touching each eye with her handkerchief, she gazes ahead, into the mist.

Soon the fog thins again to reveal a long tawny creature crouched on a tree that has toppled into the water.

"Maman," I whisper. "A mountain lion!"

"Where?"

"On that tree trunk. Drinking from the river." But even as I say these words, the fog thickens again, hiding the creature.

"You imagined it, Eugenie."

"*Non!* It was there, truly." I lower my voice, not wanting Florentine to overhear. "Mountain lions will catch Sylvette and kill her."

"Eugenie."

"We must go elsewhere, Maman. We must."

"But we cannot."

"It will be impossible here. There is nothing but forest—and wild creatures. Perhaps Indians, too."

"Not Indians, Eugenie. They have moved farther west, we have been assured. As for our dwellings, we shall have proper *maisons*. The marquis has pledged this."

"*Maisons* with stoves?"

"With hearths and stoves, surely."

"And servants?"

"Of course."

"And furnishings and beds and drapery?"

"It has all been promised."

The rain slackens, but clouds still curtain the river and mountains. The Caribbean slaves, poling the Rouleaux's boat, sing in their poor French. Our boat is silent, the rivermen grim.

"Maman?"

"Eugenie, you tire me. Allow me to rest, please."

"Just this, Maman. The Queen will come, will she not?"

"She will."

"She has escaped her captors and will come."

"Yes."

"We shall see her again."

"Of course."

"Even at this moment she may be on a ship nearing America."

"*Oui.*"

"Maman, you must speak with Papa. He cannot—"

"Eugenie, enough for now."

Then for a long while there is nothing but cloud and rain and the faint singing of the slaves. It tempts me to close my eyes and sleep, but no! I must not. *My Lady, let this day pass soon. We are cold. We have not eaten since morning.*

I hold Sylvette close and promise her a warm room and food. I do not tell her how the rain gives this day—or evening, if that is what it is—a gloomy aspect I do not at all like.

At last the Marquis de Talon stands in the boat ahead of us and gestures with his plumed hat. Our three boats begin turning toward a break in the forest on the left side of the river.

"*Mes amis,* we arrive!" the marquis calls. "Long live Marie Antoinette! Queen of France!"

Appearing along the riverbank are a number of silent figures. Maman takes my hand in hers. Sylvette looks alertly forward. Beyond the figures, a few hutlike structures appear indistinct in the mist like something in a dream.

Breath leaves me. Mama is holding herself stiffly, while Papa sags in undignified fashion against his pole. The nobles in our boat begin murmuring as our boat glides toward the landing. Then the boat is held fast and except for Florentine and us everyone else disembarks.

"I refuse to leave this boat," I am finally able to say. "The marquis must take us elsewhere."

"Eugenie," Maman says. "You are creating a scene."

"I care not! This is impossible!"

"Come now," Papa says. "We are all tired and prone to worrisome thoughts." He offers his hand.

"And famished, too," I add. "But *non!* I shall not leave until we are taken to a proper settlement."

"The mist and cloud obscure the *maisons*, Eugenie," he says after helping Maman out. "Come now."

"Papa, I am . . . afraid."

"There is nothing to fear, *chérie*."

"You do not know that for certain, Papa."

"Eugenie, you have been courageous for many weeks. Do not allow your courage to fail you now, at this moment of arrival." He offers his hand again, but I lower my head and tighten my hold on Sylvette. After a while, Papa, Maman, and Florentine leave the boat. Rivermen replace the gangplank and pull the boat, with Sylvette and me still in it, farther up onto the landing and walk off.

"Eugenie," Papa says. "Please. Let us go and find warmth."

I look at his sodden cloak and boots and almost relent, but say, "Papa, the marquis has tricked us. There is nothing here."

"Florentine," Papa says, "remain with mademoiselle, please. I shall find Talon." Florentine bows, and then Maman and Papa walk away. My heart hurts as I watch them leave. Smirking Florentine asks if I am about to pole the boat back to Philadelphia. "It will be easier, mademoiselle. The current will be in your favor."

I cannot allow him to see how fearful I am, or how angry

and hurt. When Sylvette begins whimpering, wanting to leave the boat, I extend my arm to Florentine and unsteadily step out onto a large flat stone. It seems to sway underneath us, and for a long while I can only stand there, hoping not to pitch over.

✑ *Hannah*

"Look, Hannah!" John says. "Surely, 'tis them."

A rider brought word but an hour ago, and now a canopied longboat is coming into view at the bend in the river. Two others appear behind it. Any hope that this flotilla be simply an ordinary one is fully dashed. These boats appear to hold a cargo of flowers.

Nobles. My hands begin shaking so, I have to clasp them lest my brother tease me about being scared. Broadsheet sketches show how nobles favor elaborate clothing and ornaments like silver buckles and feathers, ribbons and lace and jewelry. How they powder their hair and wear it piled up like loaves of bread. They are used to much service, Father has told us. We may oft be called upon to practice patience and charity.

"I'm counting seventeen . . . nay . . . twenty passengers," John says, "and but three cabins finished."

"Surely not thy fault, John. If thou didn't have to work so on the Queen's house, the others might be done by now."

"And even her house remains unfinished. It will go hard, I fear."

Father is standing with many of the joiners who have stopped work in order to see these nobles. They are talking among themselves and look worried. So do several of the other girls hired as servants for the French. Ten-year-old Rachel Stalk is tearing at a thumbnail with her small front

teeth. Emmeline Cooper and Mary Worthington are leaning against one another. Older women, too, clump together
like scared hens.

"John," I whisper. "We're in a real hobble, there being so
many. Dost thou think the Queen be with them?"

His jaw is hard-set, like Father's. "Could be."

"Will they take our cabin?"

"Might."

"Then how shall we do our work for them?"

"Don't know."

"Oh, John. Would that Mr. Talon had never found Father."

"He wanted the best, and Father is that."

"Aye, but all the same."

"'Tis fifty cents a day, sister."

"For thou, but twenty-five for me."

"And more for Father. We shall prosper this year, Hannah,
and earn enough for our farm."

"We know their language but poorly, John. I fear we
shan't be able to do their bidding."

"We will learn."

"And they, English?"

"They may know it already. Father says they know a great
many things despite their grand ways."

Ladies walk down the gangplank like unsteady calves. The
gentlemen do their best to keep them upright. Everyone's
feathers are drooping in the rain. All together, these nobles
look like a flock of wet fancy birds.

"John, the colors!"

"Aye."

Some ladies in rust red, others in deep green or blue.
Some in light green and pink. The loveliest paint-box colors!

The gentlemen, too. Frock coats of red and black, gold and black, blue and purple. Fur-trimmed cloaks of cranberry red and sky blue. And stockings so white. And beaver hats all beplumed. The ladies' hats, as well. It fairly takes the breath. I clasp my hands all the harder.

They are like birds that don't want to alight on the saw-dusty ground. Shaking their feathers, shaking their heads, holding up parasols, holding up gowns. Everyone is scowling. It bodes not well.

"Hannah," John says.

The tone of his voice tells me something more is amiss. And then I see the two dark-skinned men hauling up the last longboat. One is tall and thin, the other much shorter and with white hair. A Frenchman shouts at them, but they say naught. There are two other dark-skinned people in the boat, both women. One appears young. The other is stouter and older. Both are plainly dressed compared to the Frenchman, who wears a bunch of green feathers in his hat and a dark green frock coat and ember-colored cape. He is a barrel of a man, his girth making up for a lack of height.

"If they be slaves, John, Father will be most displeased." Father and Mother both have taught us that for one person to enslave another goes against the principle of equality stated so grandly in our new country's Declaration of Independence. And it goes against our own belief that there is *that of God* in each of us because each of us is made in God's image, male and female alike.

But these may be free Negroes. 'Tis possible, as there are a number of free Negroes within our Commonwealth. I pray for this to be the case, and then continue practicing the French word for *welcome.* Bienvenue. *Bee-en-ve-new.*

I survey all the ladies and decide upon the youngest, at the far end of the group. *Look kindly, Hannah, and not like a rabbit caught within a hedge of brambles.* Nobles pass us as if we aren't here at all. One corpulent noble, though, a short white beard circling jaw and chin, does glance our way. With his left hand, he holds a long walking stick for balance, but with his right, he makes some motion on the air as he passes. His mouth twitches a bit. It seems a smile. *Bee-en-ve-new,* I whisper. Now comes the young lady. She is carrying a small dog with long ears. A young man walks with her, but she is nearer to me. I am glad, for the young man appears finical.

I take a step forward. "Bien—"

The lady's face becomes a white stone, her eyes hard blue ones. She says something sharp in her language, and the finical young man gives us a look to send us under.

It startles tears. I lower my head and turn to leave, but John whispers, "Wait, Hannah. Look how they're bowing. 'Tis a sight."

Gentlemen are removing their feathered hats, taking a step backward and bowing to the ladies and to other men. Ladies hold onto their gowns, take a number of fancy steps backward, and sink downward before one another. So does the one with the white dog. The ladies, though, don't remove their high-crowned hats. The young one sets her dog down on the ground but it cries, so she lifts it up again even though its paws have gotten muddy. I might do the same, the wee thing so scared. This lady can't be as snarlish as she made herself out to be.

"John, what did I do wrong?"

"Naught, Hannah, but try to greet them. What she did was wrong. Don't blame thyself."

"Well, 'twas a poor start. Father might know. Surely I

do not wish to give such offense again." I raise my apron to my eyes.

"Ah, Hannah. They be the ones who need to learn manners."

"I fear they shall want us to bow and—"

"Well, we shan't. Father has explained it all to Mr. Talon. Do not worry so, Hannah."

"But if the Queen—which one was she, John? Dost thou know?"

"They all looked one and the same to me."

"I cannot be the one to serve her!"

"Worry not. Talon will see to it. Now I must find Father. And thou had best seek out Talon. He shall tell thee what to do. Quick, now."

He runs off in the light rain. I wish Father had not chosen me. A year. A whole year. It seems so unfair that I am weepy again. But then 'tis as if Mother is standing here alongside me, her white apron and cap glowing in the mist. *The year shall pass swiftly, dear daughter. Remember, too, that work done with love is joy.*

Mother's voice fades, but I feel warmer now, less shaky. I hold my face to the soothing rain.

Mr. Talon is calling to the girls and older women who have been hired to help. I hurry toward them.

Rushing back to our cabin, I pass Rachel, Mary, and Emmeline. Instead of getting to their tasks for the French, they are playing at curtsying before one another. "Hannah! Your Majesty!" Emmeline cries. "What shall be your bidding? I shall do it forsooth!" Grasping her gown with both hands, she bobs down, then up again, her face merry.

"Now you, Hannah!" they cry. "'Tis but a game."

I shake my head and keep going.

"Your Majesty," Mary calls. "What matter a bow if thou dost not believe in it?" They laugh. Not worried a whit.

Oh, I wish Father had picked Grace instead of me. She is but a year younger, at twelve, and so wanted to come. But Mother decided upon me because I'm older and can do more work. Grace will help Mother with the chores and with six-year-old Suzanne and watch Richard, our baby.

Thinking of Richard, his bonny cheeks and pointed nose and agreeable smile at whatever you say to him, makes tears come again. I have not seen him since July past and will not 'til July next. A year! And he shall be so different by then. He may not even remember me.

How hard it is to do what is bid thee.

I stir the venison stew and take several loaves from the warming oven. Then John and Father both enter.

"Dost thou wish thy tea?" I ask. "Or supper?"

"Hannah, daughter," Father says. "John tells me that one of the ladies was rude."

I take my chair at the table, and Father and John, theirs. "I tried to welcome her in French. It seems I did wrongly."

"Nay," Father says. "'Twas not wrong. Let us not be troubled by their bad manners. In time, perhaps, they shall learn better."

Words push forth, needing to be spoken. *They are so different from us. Could I not just take care of our house and animals and make our meals? Could not another be found to do for them?*

But I draw a long breath and remain silent so as not to offend Father.

"Hannah, remember how France came to our aid during

the war with England? Had she not, we might still be under English rule. But apart from that, 'tis our Christian duty to help these nobles, now. They've lost near everything."

Tears pinch through. I feel as if I've lost near everything, too.

"Daughter, daughter, come now." He places one hand, still cold from outside, over mine. "With our earnings this year we shall finally be able to buy our farmland. Fine valley land. No more rent that continually rises. We might even earn enough for a team of oxen. 'Tis all to the good, child, aye?"

"Aye, Father." Blinking, I keep the tears back.

"And Hannah," John says, "thou needn't have one reason in the world to be afeared of anyone who walks *thus*." He lurches on his toes from one end of our cabin to the other, Father saying, "Now, John," but smiling.

I smile, too, as I pour cups of elderberry tea for us. "Where are they to dwell, Father?"

"'Tis a problem. Talon fully sees his error—now."

"Are they still out there, in this drizzle?"

"They are, and need shelter but don't want to double up. So for some, it will have to be pine boughs and animal hides for now. John and I must leave in a trice."

"Dost thou wish they supper first?"

"Nay, not when others are doing without."

Father's words remind me how the nobles were bowing and curtsying to one another in the cold mist. One gentleman's clothing looked wet through and through and yet there he was, bowing to everyone. Most folks would rather just run somewhere dry and warm.

"They must be hungry," I finally say.

"Aye. And John, we need to build fires within the few cabins we do have. I'm told these people are quite helpless. Unlike the great La Fayette."

"Father," I ask. "Dost thou know, is the Queen among them?"

"Nay, but they expect her in the next weeks or, if not, then in the spring."

"Those others, the dark-skinned ones. Are they . . . slaves?"

Father bows his head awhile. His hair is wet. The shoulders of his deerskin jacket are wet as well. After a moment, he raises his head and regards us gravely. "Aye. Their owner is a sugar cane planter from Hispaniola. Dost thou remember thy geography, Hannah?"

"Hispaniola. 'Tis in the Caribbean Sea, to the south of our country."

"Aye. See John, our Hannah forgets naught. Well, the man has sanctuary here as well but is in a thundering tirrit at the state of things. And the unfortunate souls be bearing the brunt of his ill will. I said to Talon that we might shelter them here."

"The slave owners, Father?" John fairly shouts.

"Nay. His slaves." Father stands. "Should there be no dwelling for them, as there shan't be, I fear. John, we need—"

"Could we help them run away, Father?" I ask, the idea of it just there, bright and large.

"Hannah," John says, "art thou forgetting that law?"

And now I do remember. The Fugitive Slave Act. It was passed in February of this year by our new Congress in Philadelphia. Even though our country's Declaration of Independence states that all men are created equal and have *inalienable Rights,* many of those who signed this wonderful document turned around and wrote a law that condones slavery! Are we already snarled in hypocrisy as a nation? Father worries that we indeed are.

"These be French slaves," Father is saying. "So any law of ours may not apply to them. But now let us have a moment of quiet before we see to our tasks."

I close my eyes and a scene shapes itself around me, a grove of young maples, my favorite summer place, at home. At my feet, long thin blades of grass, curving over last year's leaves, brown and crumpled. I sit on a rock ledge and just look. The green all about gladdens my heart. So, too, the shade. The whisper of wind. My face grows warm, and my hands. I breathe in the grove's sweetness and my heart slows.

After Father and John leave, I fill a pot with stew and a basket with bread and sweet butter and prepare to carry these things to my two families, the La Roques and the Aversilles, who have been fortunate to have won, in a lottery, cabins for themselves.

As I hurry toward the new cabins, I shiver with cold and the strangeness of it all. Nobles, here. Slaves. And soon, the Queen of France.

Eugenie ॐ

Looking through the low door, I can only gasp. Our *maison* is merely a single room! Hardly even that—a mere storeroom! Still, warmth flows outward from the fire on the hearth, and so, compressing our redingotes about our traveling gowns, we dare to enter, Maman first.

Inside, we take in the rude furnishings. Gateleg table against one log wall. Candleholder and candle upon the table. Three wooden, utterly plain chairs. A peculiar small bed against the opposite wall. A bench with a high back near the fireplace. Black iron utensils to either side of the raised hearth, with wood stacked on the left. One unglazed window open to the darkness gathering outside. As workers carry in our three barrels and two trunks, Maman and I must press against one another to make room for them. When they leave, I set Sylvette down on the plank floor. At once she jumps upon the bench and sits trembling before the fire.

"We cannot stay here," I say. "We must have something better than this."

"Ah, but at least it is warm," Papa says, maneuvering around us to get to the hearth. There, he removes his wet cape and drapes it over the back of the bench. "We are fortunate, are we not, my ladies? Tonight the formidable Madame de Sevigny has only the boughs once attached to these logs."

"Perfectly appropriate, given her disloyalty," I say. "Reveling in Florentine's ignoble joke about our family crest! Poles, indeed. Still, you did bring it upon us by insisting upon poling the boat, Papa, when you needn't have. It served only to humiliate us."

"I am sorry, my Eugenie."

"Why did you, Papa?"

"For the selfish pleasure of it, I am afraid. It relieved me, for a while at least, of the burden of thought."

"While we had to bear the burden of their cruel words. How dare they, after all we have lost!"

"Ah, Eugenie, let us leave petty grievances behind. We have experienced too many grievous ones, have we not? They make all else insignificant."

Papa's play on words—*grievances, grievous*—cheers him. "This land inspires largeness, I think," he goes on.

"Tell that to Talon," Maman says, "when you see him concerning this hut, for he must do better than this. Also, please tell him that we require more candles and a lamp."

"And Papa," I add, "where is my bed? Tell him, please, that a bed for me must be brought here at once. If there is no other place for us to stay tonight, at least I must not sleep upon the floor, surely."

"Ah, *chérie*—"

"Papa, this is more wretched than any peasant's hut. At least they have something resembling beds."

I am somewhat sorry to harass him so. He is sitting before the fire, his eyes nearly shut.

"I will see about it," he says. "After dinner."

"And we can well imagine what that will be. I shall not eat it. Nor will I sleep on this so-called floor. In fact, I would prefer traveling all the way back to Philadelphia and risking the rebel sympathizers and yellow fever rather than remain here."

"Eugenie," Papa begins, but he then pauses as if thinking. Soon he is slumped against one narrow corner of the bench, dozing.

Our poor luck holds. The girl who so rudely spoke to us before first being addressed is to be one of our servants. I look down at the food she has served and anticipate being repelled, as in so many American taverns and hostelries. But to my surprise, the meat looks like meat. The carrots and potatoes, too, are identifiable. And the *ragoût* offers a fragrant aroma. Cinnamon, perhaps. To mask rancidity, no doubt. Still, I offer a *merci*, which is an invitation for her to speak, but now she remains silent.

Maman tells her not to stand there like some mule, for heaven's sake. "Curtsy!"

She remains motionless, her face quite scarlet. But after a moment she abruptly turns and leaves.

"Maman, when she comes tomorrow, we shall instruct her. Please do not be upset. She at least looks like a proper servant. Perhaps the curtsy is not an American custom."

"Well, it should be, here. This is a French settlement, where our etiquette must prevail. *Mon Dieu,* if the Queen were here . . . You are right. We shall instruct the girl, Eugenie, for the Queen's sake as well as our own. Clearly, this is a savage land, one that we must civilize."

"Far better to just leave!" I look about the room again in lingering disbelief. The Comtesse de Sevigny's harp takes up the back wall. The harpsichord Papa purchased for us in Philadelphia rests upended in a corner. Our two barrels, shoved into another corner at the foot of the bed, will have to serve as our wardrobe closet. Either that or our trunks. Intolerable! Most distressing, however, is that there is no *salle de bain,* but merely a wooden stand with a bowl and ewer upon it. And only two covered chamber pots. How humiliating. Papa shall have to request another. We do not even have a table for our *toilet* in the morning, or a mirror. All this Papa promises to discuss with the marquis. And too, the matter of the slaves being here, which we cannot tolerate.

Now Papa says, "My dear family. I have a surprise for you!"

He goes to one of the barrels in the corner, tips himself into it, rather like a duck bobbing for something in a pond, and retrieves a bottle of wine from our château. He'd wrapped it, he said, in one of our featherbeds.

Something very near joy burns away my ill mood, at least for a moment. Maman and I applaud, Maman's eyes shining with tears.

Then he pours wine into the glass goblets Talon has brought us, and we raise our goblets to the Queen and her children, Marie-Thérèse and Louis-Charles, who by this time, we pray, have been safely delivered from the ruthless rebels in France. "God grant that they arrive here soon!"

The wine tastes of our vineyard, the sun, *la France* itself. Like Maman, I cannot restrain tears.

"Let us be thankful for our deliverance," Papa is saying, "and hopeful for our future, God willing!" He takes our hands in his. "Now. Our dinner."

I am thankful for our deliverance from the rebels, but where, in my heart, is any hope? There is just disbelief, still, that this is to be our home. I touch fork to the *ragoût*. My inclination is to push it aside, but I am so hungry. Anticipating the worst, I nibble on a carrot like a timid rabbit. *Mon Dieu,* it is decent. Not overly salted at all. I try another. The same! Then for the true test—the meat. Eyes closed, I raise a tiny bit to my mouth. I chew, swallow, and then open my eyes to meet Maman's.

"*C'est bon!*" Maman exclaims.

We each take another forkful while Papa eats like one starved. The *ragoût* is not merely good but excellent. Sylvette is frantic for the bits of meat I give her. Our new servant has brought bread as well and it, too, is delicious, with its sweet butter. "You see?" Papa says. "All will be well yet, my ladies."

After we finish, Maman asks, "But where is our servant?"

We look to the closed door.

"The plates must be removed and washed."

Papa offers to do it. There is hot water in a pot hanging in the fireplace.

"*Non!*" Maman says. "In the morning she will do it—after she curtsies three times to each of us to make up for her insolence tonight."

Insolence? Perhaps, yes. She frightens me, this servant, for in her eyes I see the stubbornness and antipathy of our peasants. Yet she is a commendable cook, if she has indeed made the meal herself.

"But where are our other servants?" I ask. "And how shall I sleep tonight, without a bed?"

"Eugenie," Papa says, "tonight you must encamp upon the floor. I will get your featherbed for you, though no rugged campaigner has ever had that luxury."

"Forgive me, Papa, but I am not a campaigner. I cannot sleep upon a floor, even if upon feathers. I must have a bed."

"And where are we to find such an object this night, my lady?"

"I do not know! We must, though."

Papa goes to our one door and opens it wide to wind and heavy rain. "Bonsoir, bonsoir! Does anyone have an extra bed out there? No? Not tonight?"

He closes the door. "A pity. No beds."

I laugh despite myself. "Papa! No one could possibly hear you."

"Well, but we do have the bench."

"It will be too hard."

He regards it. "So it will. And too narrow."

Again he goes to one of our barrels and this time pulls out another of our featherbeds, which he places upon the floor before the hearth.

"Papa, I cannot sleep there."

"But it is the finest place in our *maison*. Certainly the warmest."

Sylvette goes to the featherbed and curls up on it.

"Voilà! The creature is intelligent, no?"

"Where shall I change my clothing? Where shall I hang things? This is impossible. You must discuss it all with Talon tonight."

"Tonight, my lady?"

"Of course," Maman says. "And why not demand that he provide a *maison* more conducive to civilization."

"*Oui,*" I say. "A wonderful idea. And you did promise to take it all up with him, Papa."

"Did I? Perhaps I was talking in my sleep." He puts on his still-wet cloak.

"Papa, wait. Perhaps in a while the rain will—"

"*Non, non!* It will take but a minute."

"Well, then, do not forget the matter of the slaves, either. They may be harboring the yellow fever that has been plaguing Philadelphia."

And then he is gone. As Maman and I change into our nightgowns, cold and revulsion make me shudder. *This, our home?*

There is nothing to be done for now, Papa tells us when he returns, except to lower the piece of leather over our one unglazed window and keep close to the fire. As for returning to Philadelphia, that would be most unwise. Apart from the great number of American anti-Loyalists there—for after all, did not the American revolution inspire the French rebels?—French anti-Loyalists may have followed us to America with deadly intent. Papa's voice has sunk to a near whisper, as if he does not wish to give voice to old worries in this new land.

The marquis, he goes on, promises that workers shall build us an extra bed as soon as they can. Later, they may even be able to enlarge our *maison* by adding a wing and then cutting a door through one of our walls. And then, soon after that, furniture shall be delivered from Philadelphia to make our new home more habitable.

But I know about the marquis's promises.

"Papa, forgive me, but it is unacceptable. I must at least have a bed."

His eyes are reddened and sleepy, even mournful now, and there are purple indentations underneath them. Still, I persist, though it shames me to do so. "Papa? At least that much?"

He draws a long breath and slowly exhales. "Eugenie," he begins. Then he pauses for some time. Always before, he has been able to grant my every wish.

"You may, then, have that one," he says finally, pointing to the room's small bed. "Your mother and I shall . . ." Wearily, he looks toward the hearth.

Tonight my bedchamber is this, our common room. Lying here, on the floor, it seems that I am still on some swaying, dipping boat. My eyes close, but then I am seeing—yet again!—my beloved Annette in that farm cart, peasants thronged behind and all around, shouting. I open my eyes upon the dying fire on the hearth. My heart is beating fearfully. My breath comes too fast. "Sylvette," I whisper. "Where are you?"

My hands cup her warm leathery paws as another scene forms, in memory.

Eugenie! Don't stand there. Take one thing and come. Bernard is ready with the coach. Hurry! I look about my room. The great windows are open, the air sweet with late summer. Maman's gaze follows mine.

The servants will close them. Come, come!

I scoop Sylvette up.

Leave her, Eugenie! We cannot take a dog. It will be too dangerous.

Then I cannot go. I will stay with Louisa and Bernard.

Then you will die here!

I cannot leave Sylvette. I will not. I know I must leave Henriette. I cannot take my horse, and now they will kill her.

They will not kill a mare. She is too useful.

Sylvette is not useful, so they shall kill her just as they did Annette. I will not leave her, Maman.

How dare you do this now, Eugenie.

I am sorry, Maman. I cannot leave her. You said to take one thing. I am taking Sylvette—or staying.

You stubborn girl, then hurry. We cannot remain here any longer. Bernard said . . .

What, Maman?

That we must go. Quickly! Quickly!

Turning my head from the fire, now, I cling to Sylvette and she, it seems, to me. But I dare not close my eyes again.

The rain sounds like applause that goes on and on.

⟡ *Hannah*

Still abed—at seven in the morning? I use the stone knocker again. After a long while, Comte de La Roque unbars the door. His wig is low upon his forehead, his eyes a sore red. He doesn't know who I am, at first.

I don't open my mouth, though. Learnt that lesson yesterday. I show him the porridge, bacon, and coffee. He shakes his head and says something in French. Perhaps he means for me to come later. I raise the pole, with my pots, and turn to leave.

"Non!" he says. *"Entrez–vous!"* He curves his arms and motions. *"Entrez, entrez!"*

Inside is a regular Hurra's nest. Dirty plates and fancy glass upon the fine white cloth that covers the table. Well, 'tis my fault, that. Clothing everywhere about, and some of it still wet. The fire mere ashes.

I step 'round the young lady sleeping on a makeshift bed on the floor near the hearth. Her little dog sits up to watch me. Sweet thing! Ears like mittens. Would that I could touch one.

· *Thou musn't, Hannah!*

Now a bit of tinder to the ashes, and a few bits of kindling, and there it is, the fire cracklin' nicely. I make a tepee of logs, and it's soon full blazes.

Porridge pot gets set on a trivet amid some warm ashes. Coffee pot on another. The plate of bread and bacon goes on the warm hearthstone.

Ah, she's a pretty lass, the young one. Yellow hair all a'fluff. Her face not so sickly white as yesterday. And a lot younger than I thought. More Grace's age, or even my own. And here I was thinking she was a lady. Mayhap the meanness made her look older.

Quiet, I gather up the plates, each thin as a flower petal and blue as a summer's sky rimmed with white cloud. I wish Mother could see them. She'd like the pictures of flowers inside the white, roses and something yellow linked by little leaves. Last night I paid them no heed. 'Tis a wonder I didn't smash one with my ladle, scared as I was.

Well, my hands are still trembly. *Careful, Hannah!* The water has gone cold, so I carry the plates back to our cabin. Don't know but we'd best get the La Roque family some sturdy pewter plates and porrigers. These mightn't last the week.

One thing at a time! Don't let thoughts race on so, for they'll surely outrun you. Now get these nobles their breakfast, and they might cheer, some.

It cheers me, at least, to see them all up and dressed when I return with the washed plates. So that much they can do for themselves, anyway.

No mugs for coffee?

Back I go. The wind has come up now, out of the northwest. Mr. Talon does not understand wind in the least. First he had all the big trees cut and the stumps burnt out. Then he made the wide avenues and had a few cabins built along them. Playthings for the wind is all. And those avenues a place for it to rampage. I lower my chin and push against it.

Our cabin is tucked away in the trees on the north side of the clearing. Other workers built their cabins at the fringe of woods, too. The trees behind us stop the wind from its games, but the sun can still find us when the leaves are down.

From our cupboard I take three mugs from a set made by my uncle Gearson at his pottery in Wilkes-Barre. In shape they are quite simple, with wide bases and narrower tops and pleasantly curved handles. The color is a warm oaken brown. I consider them handsome and hope they will not offend.

The La Roques find naught to complain about while they eat their breakfast. I step back from their table to await further orders and soon find myself staring at two objects I failed to notice last night, in my fear. A golden harp, reaching the ceiling, nearly. And next to it, another instrument I know only from pictures in books—a harpsichord.

Oh, Hannah, to think you may soon hear music from these instruments!

I am fair shivery with the thought.

The Aversille cabin is across the main avenue, but it takes a hundred paces to get there. Imagine—a road one hundred paces wide! The cabin was supposed to be the priest's, but he gave it up to the elderly Aversilles. Father had much to say in praise of this.

Comte d'Aversille opens his door and says a string of French words that scorch my face. I try to read his expression, but he is an old man, and the wrinkles are all settled into a frown. There is a hump to his back. He's wearing a white wig with three rows of curls on each side and a little tail in back tied with a black ribbon. His frock coat holds a pattern of crimson roses on a black background. He looks like a judge. Madame d'Aversille sits at the table with a fan in her right hand. She has on a fur-trimmed cloak over her gown. She also wears a white wig with curls like piled-up logs.

While I build up their fire, I wonder if the French people know how to smile or whether 'tis not customary. Madame d'Aversille's wrinkles all droop down into a frown, too. Maybe after so much frowning, the skin just hardens in those ridges, like the clay we play with in Uncle's pottery.

But look, Hannah, someone here has washed up their dishes!

These are fetching, too. White with a rose border. The French people must like flowers, so maybe they are not so mean as they act. But pretty or no, these plates are none deep enough.

After serving the Aversilles, I ask in my poor French if there be anything else they need.

More frowning.

I leave, not knowing if there is or isn't. Still, 'tis something that one of them washed those dishes.

I wish I had been assigned to Abbé La Barre. *Abbé*, I have just learned, is a French word for *priest*. But little Rachel Stalk is to be his servant. He seems a good man, the way he gave up the cabin he won in the lottery and asked for a chapel to be built before any house for himself. There he is now, sprinkling water over wickets and cabins alike. Huffing, he walks as if his legs pain him and there isn't enough breath within the whole of him to get him where he needs go. So he stops often and leans on his stick, his great chest heaving. Black fur lines his black cloak, but his hat is such as rivermen wear—wide-brimmed leather. He is using a sprig of white pine and dipping it into a bucket he himself carries. All the while he says words in a strange language, not French but something different. Perhaps 'tis a prayer.

It seems so unjust for the cross-grained slave owner to have a cabin but not the priest.

At one of the wickets, the youngest slave comes out and kneels at his feet. She bows her head, and the priest sprinkles her with water, too. She wears neither jacket nor cloak. 'Tis a most troubling sight. I am a few steps beyond them when the slave owner shouts, and the girl gets quickly to her feet. The owner points to the woods, and then returns to his cabin. The slave girl walks toward the woods just as she is, in her cotton gown, while the priest leaves to sprinkle other places. I fear that she will lose her way in the woods, and so I follow. A few paces into the forest, she stops and merely stands there. Then she raises both hands to her eyes and covers them.

"*Pardonnez-moi,* mademoiselle," I say, and she swings around, scared as anything. But I can only say, in French, *How may I help you?* Without relaxing, she leans down and picks up a long dry branch and begins pulling it toward the clearing.

Firewood.

I find another and pull it to the clearing, too. Soon we have a pile. She begins breaking one up, using her feet. But at the branch's thick end, she cannot. Nor can I. She wears no shoes, just wet muddy cloth wrapped around each foot. She gathers an armful of the small pieces, and I gather one, too. But her master appears and shouts in French at both of us. She backs away from him and runs to the forest again.

I hurry to the half-finished cabin where Father and John

are at work and tell them about the girl. They each take up saws, and we rush back to the place. There, the younger of the two dark men is with the girl now—his face is a jumble of lumpy scars, and his right eye is all but closed. He bows and she curtsies, but Father shakes his head. Then he and John carry more tree limbs out and saw them up as if possessed by Furies. The slaves wear neither shoes nor boots, just those mud-clumped rags. Their mouths shake with cold.

As we walk away, Father tells us he learned just that morning that Mr. Rouleau doesn't want them under a proper roof when some of the nobles have to do without. As for the nobles, none of them wished to stay with us. Nor—strangest of all—did they want our cabin because we have been living there.

For this, anyway, I am grateful.

"Why don't the slaves just leave him," I ask. "They could run into these woods, hide, and—"

"Ah, Hannah, they know not these woods. They speak not our language. A bounty will be posted and whoever does help them . . . well, 'twill go hard."

Aye. That law. The fine is five hundred dollars. And if 'tis a person of color who tries to help—a free man or woman—that person will be sold into servitude as punishment if the fine cannot be paid.

"Even here in Pennsylvania," John says, "where there's not supposed to be slaves?"

"That I know not," Father says. "But 'tis possible."

"At least we might help them to keep warm," I say.

"Aye," Father says quietly.

"But if we do, will it be breaking some law?"

"It may, here."

I am fairly hobbled by the thought of a law against helping folk.

Madame de La Roque says something harsh in French, I know not what. Heat again stings my face. But then she curtsies before me! I back away from her. She raises her voice and says something more in French. Then curtsies again.

I am nearly at the door. She comes close and places her hands on my shoulders and presses down.

She wants you to curtsy to her, Hannah.

I take another step backward. Her hands slip off. French words pour around me. The pink of her skin deepens. Her eyes narrow. She points toward her daughter, and then toward Comte de La Roque and finally to herself. Again she drops low before me and looks like a swan, the way her neck curves. Then once more she points to me.

I shake my head. *"S'il vous plaît, pardonnez-moi!"* I want to run, but there are the dishes on the table. If I don't get them now, I'll have to return soon.

Quick, I dash around her, grab up the dishes, dash around her yet again, and then am outside, in the wind.

At our cabin, I'm surprised to find John there, leaning over a length of cherry plank set up on sawhorses. He is smoothing out the plank's roughness with a hand plane. The marquis, he says, has ordered him to make a bed.

"But I thought thou must work on the cabins." My voice is still shaky, and my hands.

"First, this."

"Who is it for?"

"He did not say."

Holding the plates with my other hand, I take up a curl of paper-thin wood spilling from the plane. The curl is nearly white, its scent calming. When the wood is oiled it will turn a golden pink, and then, in time, a deep red. I envy John his skill and often wish that I, too, had been taught to work with wood. Does he envy my ability to make bread?

I needn't even bother to ask!

It takes all the courage I possess to return to the La Roques' cabin with their supper and the clean plates. Marquis Talon is there. He tells me, in English, that I must never speak to a French noble unless one first speaks to me, inviting some response. Also, I must curtsy each time I enter a noble's house and before I leave and anytime I come upon one. He asks where I was yesterday when he gave these instructions to all the serving girls, but he does not pause for me to reply. And because I did not curtsy last night, I must do so three times, now, to each of the La Roques. "Begin!"

"I am sorry, sir, but I . . . cannot."

"And why is that? Do you have some infirmity?"

"Nay. We believe . . . sir . . . 'tis our religion that . . . forgive me, I speak poorly."

"You ask that I forgive your speech but not your actions?"

"We believe . . . we believe that all are equal in the sight of God. We do not place ourselves above others . . . or . . . below. 'Tis our . . . religion."

"Yes. *Quakers.* Your father did tell me this." He rapidly shakes his head as some do to mock us. "A sect! Not a proper religion at all!"

"We call ourselves Friends. The Society of Friends."

"Religion or not, I have decided that it is now necessary for you to curtsy and for your father and brother to bow when any noble approaches."

"But thou did not—"

"I forbid you to address me as an equal. This is not a discussion. What is now is now. And you must not speak until first spoken to by a noble. It is for us to decide whether or not we wish to hear your voice."

"General Washington," I begin, but then stop.

"What about your president?"

Am I being invited to speak? It seems so. "He does not bow to royalty."

"Ah! You impertinent child! You are not General Washington, are you?"

I stand there, mute.

"Answer me when I require an answer. Are you General Washington?"

"No, Mr. Talon."

"Henceforth address me properly. I am a marquis!"

"No, Mr. Marquis."

"Not *mister*, child! Do you not know anything? Call me . . . *Excellency*. Do you understand?"

"Yes . . . Excellency."

"*Bon.* Now curtsy."

I stand there trembling. I can fairly see my hands leaping about.

"Curtsy!"

I lower my head further. Marquis Talon's face has become almost violet, as if all this is bruising him. What mine must look like I do not wish to guess.

"*Pardonnez-moi,*" I whisper.

He swings away from me, his cape whipping about and all but taking my apron. "I go to speak to your father. Remain outside."

The desire to run is so strong that I must grab hold of a log sticking out from a corner of the cabin. For, surely, if I disobey, it will go hard on Father and John. At last there he is, the marquis, striding toward me, his cloak blowing back from his frock coat. Three gray feathers in the band of his high-crowned hat bob in the wind. His dark eyes are those of a hawk diving upon its prey. His face is still fairly violet.

"Hannah Kimbrell, enter the *maison*."

I do so.

He speaks in French and then in English, telling me that he has no choice but to fine us for our insubordination. Each time I do not curtsy—or Father and John do not bow—it will cost a penny. The fines shall be taken from our earnings at the end of each month.

"What say you to this, Hannah Kimbrell?"

"If it be what my father wishes, then it must be so."

"And you? Would you not prefer to put aside the money for your farm? Oh, yes, I know all about this. Your father has told me. If you choose to curtsy, Hannah Kimbrell, you will be helping your family. Do you see that? Not hindering."

"I wish . . . to obey my father."

"So be it. We shall keep tally. And so shall every other French nobleman and lady within the settlement. Those present now and those still to arrive. And so shall I, beginning immediately. Curtsy, Hannah Kimbrell."

I stand there.

"One penny, then." He extends his gloved hand.

"I do not have it."

"Well, I shall mark it. And so shall the La Roque family. I give you one more chance. Curtsy!"

The door is two paces behind him. I hurry to it, squeeze myself through, and am out in open air, running.

"Father! They shall drain away our earnings with this rule."

"They shall cut into it, surely."

"Is it worth even staying, then?"

"Aye. There will be some profit."

"Enough to purchase our farm?"

"Perhaps."

"But can we believe their tallies? Or will Mr. Talon just . . . use any number so long as it is high, each month? Why is he like this, now? It was all right with him before! Is it because the nobles are here? When he wanted thou, he said we needn't—"

"Hannah, Hannah. Take a breath, daughter."

"Oh, Father, can we not go home?"

"We gave our word."

"Could thou not stop work until—"

"'Tis not just to meet wrong with wrong, my Hannah."

"But will they come to see the wrong of it? I think not!"

"Then they will not."

"But our farm!"

"Then we shall find another way."

"And this year will be for naught."

"Things are never for naught. Perhaps in time thou shall see this for thyself. Now let us reflect."

Closing my eyes, I see, at first, only Mr. Talon's violet face, his black eyes. I hear only his storm of words. That fades and I am reflecting upon home—rocking bonny Richard and singing the counting song to him while a good fire burns on the hearth and Mother and Grace shell the last beans from our garden.

Peace does not come. Only longing.

Eugenie 🍂

The afternoon is quite warm, with thick white clouds filled with light. These great sails skim the mountaintop across the river and move swiftly on. Would that I could go with them! Everything seems in motion. Clouds. River. Leaves. They tear away from ancient oaks, fly with the wind, then swoop down en masse and rush along the avenue, only to rise again in whirlwinds Sylvette chases.

"*Ma petite,*" I call. "Do not become too accustomed to this place, now! Our true home is in France!" At my voice Sylvette turns and begins barking. I envision some wild animal's approach and swing around to face—

Only a team of horses and a wagon. Well, I shall not give way and move to the side. What is a mere wagon to a French noble? I continue walking, but the clattering wagon brings that darker image of farm cart and peasants taking my Annette away, and fear spirals through me like those leaves.

The wagon stops—this I hear, and then cannot resist the temptation to turn again. A team of two great Belgian horses is pulling a load of logs. Or rather, has been, for now the horses stand there, flicking their long, plumelike tails and regarding me. One stamps a foreleg, with its cone of feathery "mane" covering its pastern. In the wagon's seat are two men, one older and the other young. The younger one jumps down and, perhaps afraid that Sylvette's barking shall unnerve the horses, goes to one of them and holds its harness.

He is dressed like a republican in a dark coat and trousers, with a white linen shirt and black hat. His unpowdered hair is held back with a simple tie. Despite his appearance, I am so relieved not to see a farm cart. "Sylvette, hush, *ma petite*. Do you not remember what horses look like?" I pick her up and walk closer. It seems years since I have been this near beautiful horses. Their manes and tails are the color of fresh cream. The flounce of mane falling over their pasterns, too. Their coats remind me of hazelnuts. And their harness looks clean and supple. The young man keeps hold of the horse as I reach up to touch its great dark muzzle. Ah! The warmth! The petal softness! A horse's muzzle has never failed to astonish and delight me. Tears come, for this huge horse suddenly becomes my little Henriette.

But the young man ruins it all by addressing me in English.

"How impertinent!" I tell him in French. "I did not address you, did I?" It is gratifying to see him step backward as if struck.

I walk on toward the river, and the road behind me remains quiet. Perhaps they are afraid, now, to pass, as well they should be.

At the river there are no boats to be seen anywhere except for the small skiff tied at the landing farther down the bank of the river. I watch the water for a while. I toss a stick for Sylvette. She retrieves it, but lets it fall in order to bark at Florentine du Vallier's approach.

Ignoring Sylvette, Florentine throws a stone far into the

river. Sylvette sees the splash and whimpers. I take hold of her ribbon leash.

"*Bon matin*, Mademoiselle de La Roque!" He executes a deep bow, but I offer only a preemptory curtsy in response. "So here we are, then!" he says. "Throwing stones and sticks. What grand amusement, no?"

Florentine rarely smiles with anything like pleasure. Usually he grimaces. Possibly his teeth hurt him. But whatever the reason, the grimace does make him seem older than his sixteen years. Even at Versailles he found much to complain about. With Florentine one must remember not to be enthusiastic about anything. That only invites his derision.

I imitate his sarcastic tone. "A good day for throwing things, anyway."

He offers his grimace and continues making distant splashes in the pewter-colored water. I keep tight hold of Sylvette.

"So what do you think of our *grandes châteaux?*" he asks.

"Hmmm . . ." I pretend to be thinking, but it truly is a difficult question to answer successfully. After visiting Madame de Sevigny in her poor hut of pine boughs and animal hides, I realized that we have been fortunate in the lottery despite the rudeness of everything. But to admit this won't do. Either I must be witty or scornful, and best if I can be both, a talent much admired at court. "Such a place thwarts thinking," I say finally. *"Non?"*

He laughs, but the successful parry gives me little pleasure. I wish I could ask how he feels, truly feels, about this place and about everything that has happened to us. Jest, witticisms now seem so irrelevant.

"Florentine—I say," but he, too, has begun to speak, begging pardon for the witticism he made at Papa's expense the day we arrived.

"It was nothing," I say, offering my own dart.

"We all found ourselves admiring your father's strength. We placed wagers on when he might tire and stop. No one won, mademoiselle. Remarkable!"

How dare they. "Ah, yes. Papa is a man of many surprises."

"Indeed! It seems that now, instead of the river, he is testing his strength against the wood of these mountains."

"We find it remarkable as well."

"I daresay so shall Marie Antoinette."

"Do you know, Florentine, you are quite right! She shall! We all know of her tenderness toward our late king, a man of great practical skills."

I recall how our late king loved to tinker with locks, a skill not unlike joinery. And when he was younger, he'd go off somewhere in old clothes and work alongside common stonemasons, erecting walls. Courtiers laughed behind his back and called him eccentric, or worse. Which is exactly what we fear for Papa.

Florentine hides his displeasure at my triumph by turning to the river. Then Sylvette is barking at the clouds, her neck straining upward.

"What is it, *chérie?*"

Other barking echoes hers, coming from above, in the sky. *Saperlotte!* Lines of wild geese flying low, under the clouds! And they are all barking like little Sylvettes. Where do they come from? Where do they go? South, it must be. Perhaps following the river to Philadelphia and beyond. Florentine pretends to aim a gun and shoot at them.

Hannah Kimbrell appears and, ignoring Talon's earlier lesson, addresses us first.

"Excusez-moi. C'est pour Sylvette."

Florentine sweeps his hands outward. "How dare you! Away with you, insolent girl. I have heard about you and see that you still do not curtsy. I shall inform the marquis at once."

His tone is so venomous that I find myself blushing in annoyance and almost siding with the girl.

"Ah!" I say and laugh. "I believe she meant to address the dog, not us, Florentine. You see? She has something for Sylvette." Hoping to divert his attention, I quickly unfold the piece of broadsheet.

"It does not excuse disrespect."

"Indeed, Florentine, but look. A bone for Sylvette!"

"I care not if it is a diamond collar. She must pay for her effrontery."

Sylvette diverts me from my own anger at the girl. She dances. She stands balanced on her hind legs. She hops straight upward and then drops to the ground and begins gnawing on the bone. I have never seen her so happy in this America. But then Hannah Kimbrell stoops to stroke her fur, and I pull at the ribbon leash. Sylvette topples backward.

"You Americans," Florentine rants on in French. "You are all barbarians. I'm surprised you do not wear bones in your noses as well as carry them about with you."

True. And yet—

"The impertinent girl must be punished," Florentine is saying.

"Florentine, she understands neither your words nor your wit."

"She soon shall!"

"Yes, of course. My dear Florentine, you are right. It is unforgivable of her to approach us like that, and with a bone, no less. But see how happy it has made poor Sylvette? She hasn't had such a treasure since we left France. If Talon hears of this, then it will be hardest on Sylvette. The girl is quite taken with her and no doubt will bring her other gifts—if we do not interfere. Will you not desist for Sylvette's sake?"

"And yours, mademoiselle?" he asks with sly innuendo.

"Of course! What is good for Sylvette is good for me as well."

It is the closest I've ever come to speaking truthfully with Florentine. I fear, though, that in my truthfulness, I am quite misleading him. A fine irony, no?

"Allow me to escort you back to your *maison*, lest any other barbarians decide to take advantage of a lady's vulnerability."

Vulnerability. Weakness. It must be true, for look—I am incapable even of extricating myself from his presence. Hannah Kimbrell has moved smoothly away, swift as the American Indians of stories, while I totter alongside Florentine like a child.

Shouts come from somewhere nearby. "The Queen?" I cry. "She arrives?" But the voice seems to be saying *Stop!*

"We must learn what it is!" Florentine pulls me in the direction of the shouting.

It is only the boorish slave owner, Rouleau. And there are the horses, the wagon, and the two men, all of them at the edge of the forest, not far from the river.

"Kimbrell, I warn you," Rouleau shouts in French. "Whatever you build here, I shall pull down. They are not to have a shelter to best the nobles'. Do you understand me?"

I doubt that either of them does. They continue unloading logs while Rouleau rages. "It will give them ideas. It is dangerous, Kimbrell. What they have now is good enough."

Then, as if it has been emerging from the forest all this while, I finally see a green hut, not unlike Madame de Sevigny's. Its roof and sides have been formed by boughs of pine and fir. A small cooking fire burns before it, and the white-haired slave woman emerges from the hut with a pot in hand. Her gown is of some thin and faded cotton, and she wears an equally thin half cape over her shoulders. Seeing us, she pauses in her work to curtsy.

"If you persist, Kimbrell," Rouleau is saying, "I shall whip my slaves for each day you dare to come here. Beginning today."

Whip them? For something they themselves do not do?

Kimbrell. The young man's name—and Hannah's. They must be brother and sister, for I see a resemblance in the dark hair, dark eyes, and fair skin. The older man must be their father—and the one Papa has been working with on the chapel.

"*Excusez-moi,* Monsieur Rouleau," I call. "They do not understand French. They are but ignorant Americans."

Rouleau bows before replying. "Whether they understand or not, mademoiselle, is not your affair."

Florentine stiffens at this insult yet does nothing other than lead me away. Of course—he is afraid of the man and his whip.

I decide to tell Papa of this matter, and then Papa can inform the marquis, and the marquis will relay word to the Kimbrells.

But the four slaves are whipped by Rouleau. It is some three hours later, and Florentine has come to tell us about it, reveling in the news. Maman turns her head to the side and says nothing, a subtle expression of displeasure lost upon Florentine. Papa regards Florentine with reserve. This afternoon Talon told Papa that we must not interfere in Rouleau's affairs.

"Is he not a citizen of France?" Papa asked. "And thus answerable to us for his treatment of the slaves?"

Talon merely said, "What is all this concern about his slaves? Besides, Rouleau is right. We must first have *maisons* for our own people. I, too, have forbidden the Kimbrells to work on a *maison* for the slaves when I need them to do so much else. But they are meddlesome, I fear, and no doubt will continue."

"They must be told about the whippings," Papa said.

"Let them find out on their own, and be sorry for it. Maybe that will stop them."

Now I am near sickened, imagining these whippings, and yet . . . surely it is not right for slaves to have a *maison* before Madame de Sevigny does. "You see all the trouble these slaves bring!" I cannot help saying. "They should not be here at all. I have thought this all along. It is Talon's fault—and Noailles's."

"Indeed," Florentine says, offering his smirk.

It disgusts me, Florentine trying to ally himself with me. I give him a look and refuse to say anything further until after he leaves.

"Papa. You must inform the Kimbrells. I do not think people should be whipped for something they do not do."

Maman and Papa regard me.

"Well? I speak truly, do I not?"

"Your father must not interfere, Eugenie. We are here at the marquis's pleasure. And Noailles's."

After playing the harpsichord, as Maman requested, I write a note in simple French, telling Hannah about the whippings. I plan to quickly tuck it into her apron pocket when she serves us this evening. But a different American girl comes with a steaming pot and, after curtsying, clumsily fills our bowls with some gray potage. I stare at it. A fish head rises to the surface and stares back. *Mon Dieu!* Then the girl places a scorched piece of yellow bread to one side of the bowl. Her ragged fingernails are dark with dried blood. Her fingers are dirty. I look at Maman. Her chin is high. Her eyes appear to notice nothing amiss. After the girl curtsies and leaves, with her ill-smelling pot, Maman says, "I do not wish to keep a tally. I do not wish to witness Hannah Kimbrell's discomfort day after day when I have enough of my own to occupy me. We demanded satisfaction from Talon and received it. *Bon.* Now we shall have the respect due our rank." She sips a spoonful of the potage and after a moment swallows. Slowly, she dips her spoon again. Papa, saying nothing, eats.

Fish-head soup. High price to pay for respect, no?

The bread is inedible. The potage—I give mine to Sylvette. Even she hesitates. Soon after, I retreat to my featherbed by the hearth. The fire snaps and flickers. I cannot bear to look at it. But when I close my eyes, I am again encased within the roll of Italian velvet, stifling, airless, being smuggled onto the merchantman ship.

Sleep seems impossible. The odor of that potage still per-
meates the *maison*. I take the note from under the featherbed. How shall I get it to her?

The night is long. In time, a plan forms.

Hannah

"Chantez, chantez," Madame d'Aversille commands.

I sing, for the hundredth time, it seems, the old counting song "Over in the Meadow." *Over in the meadow in the sand in the sun, lived an old mother turtle and her little turtle one. "Dig," said the mother. "I dig," said the one. So he dug and was glad in the sand in the sun.* On and on, all ten verses in English, but still madame touches each eye with her lacy handkerchief. When I finish, madame takes up a quill, makes three marks on her tally, then strikes through them. She holds up the paper for me to see. I smile a little, for she is grinning like a mischievous child.

But why make the marks at all, then? These French people truly are a puzzle.

Madame d'Aversille sighs and leans back in her straight chair. Her feet rest upon the pillow of lamb's wool I made for her. Her eyes are half-closed, yet she draws the sheet nearer to her elbow and makes yet another mark but does not strike through it.

Then she gives me a wide smile. 'Tis like young Richard's, if I could erase the wrinkles. She says something in French and draws her arm through the air. She says something more in French. Is she having a talk with herself? I wish I knew what about.

Now she groans and points to her head.

The wig, Hannah?

I am afraid to move. She points again and pulls at the thing. It seems stuck there. Possum holding fast by its tail.

I go behind her chair and lift it away, but then do not know what to do with it. Finally I hang it on the other chair. She looks so old and tired now. Her own bit of hair is stuck damply to her scalp like the few feathers on a chick just come out of an egg, all crumpled and wet. I do the only thing I can think of, then. I dip a cloth in the basin and dab her head and the few strands of hair. I pat her head dry and comb the wisps straight back.

"Ah! *Merci, merci!*"

I wash the damp powder from her face. Dab away the tears gathering at the withered corners of her eyes.

"*Chantez,*" she says again. "*Chantez!*"

In the middle of the second verse comes a tapping at the door. Visitors? I hurriedly replace her wig, but 'tis on crooked! "*Entrez!*" Madame calls, eager, it seems, for this new diversion. I step well back as the door opens.

Mademoiselle de La Roque enters, with her little dog. Seeing me, it barks and barks. When she sets it down, it runs to me and keeps hopping up. Madame d'Aversille laughs and claps her hands. She calls to the dog in quick French, and finally it goes to her. She picks it up and holds it against her wrinkled face. The dog squirms but then begins licking her face. Madame laughs some more. So does mademoiselle. I move farther back, awaiting the order to curtsy, and the new tally marks.

Mademoiselle looks at the table, its teapot and the apple tart I baked, and madame notices. She is like a cat that way, missing nothing. "*Mangez!*" she commands. Then, "Ha-nah!"

Trembly, I serve mademoiselle while the two talk. Their

words seem the crackling of bird chatter. Every so often madame looks at me and grins. Listening to mademoiselle, she shakes her head. And all the while, mademoiselle eats like one starved. Three pieces of tart with cream! Finally madame says, *"Chantez,* Ha-nah! *Chantez!"*

I do not wish to sing! I wish to flee to my own cabin. This day will cost a dozen marks.

"Ha-nah!"

I sing for them seven verses, in English, of the counting song. Mademoiselle listens but does not look at me.

Then, there's more talk in French. So far neither one has made a mark on the tally sheet. But finally, mademoiselle stands and calls to her dog. Madame taps, with crooked index finger, the tally sheet. Mademoiselle looks from it to me and makes a mark, but madame crosses through it and laughs. Mademoiselle tries to make another. Madame brushes her hand away.

Seems a game, Hannah. I am happy for madame, at least, for most days she is a sad, broody creature. And today is dark, with wind.

As she throws on her cape, mademoiselle gestures for me to approach. When I do, she leans down and, quick, catches up her dog. But just before that, she tucks something into my apron pocket. There is no way to see what it is because madame has other things for me to do. While I work, I hear someone playing the harpsichord at the La Roques' cabin. Could it be mademoiselle? 'Tis a sprightly tune, quick and lively, and madame taps a foot. In the sound I see a field full of wildflowers in sun and wind. Pink mallow and buttercups and black-eyed Susan and daisies and red clover, all swaying and bright.

To be able to make such music, Hannah!
My arms prickle at the thought.

A note, I see later, while madame naps. A few words come clear—*Papa . . . maison . . . nègre . . .* My heart fair stumbles as I try to guess at the meaning. I will need our dictionary.

Eugenie

We have survived yet another night in this wilderness. And here is another day to traverse. And Florentine again here, a clinging vine. We walk, and he talks, and while he talks, I give attention to other thoughts—Hannah and the note I delivered successfully. And quick upon that thought, another—Kimbrell fils. I am somewhat ashamed of myself for berating him as I did when he stopped with that team of horses. Then as if my thoughts have the power to summon that young man, two workers appear on the avenue, carrying something—to our *maison!* Heat floods my face, for the object is a bed. And the younger of the two men is indeed Kimbrel fils.

"Such wood to be had, here?" I exclaim, as if this alone has made color rush to my face. The smooth wood of the rails appears more like the finest satin.

"What is truly remarkable, mademoiselle, is that they do not set down their burden and acknowledge our presence. I must learn their names."

Florentine releases my arm and prepares to do battle. *"Arretez-vous!"*

"Florentine, allow them to continue, please. They are bringing that for me."

"Do you know them? They seem—but of course! Are they not the ones who attempted to build a *maison* for the slaves?"

Again he orders them to stop, but they pay no heed. The

young man lets the river stone fall against our door, and Papa opens it.

"Comte," Florentine says, standing ignominiously behind the workers, "I must learn their names. They refused to bow."

"Ah! Florentine." Papa executes a bow, which Florentine returns. Then Papa steps aside and the workers enter. First they remove Madame de Sevigny's harp, and then they place the new bed against the far wall, opposite the hearth. Kimbrell père offers me something wrapped, like Sylvette's bone, in broadsheet paper.

"Do not accept it!" Florentine urges. But I open the parcel and find panels of cream-colored muslin and a length of cord. Kimbrell père gestures to the ceiling, takes hooks and hammer from a pouch, and soon the two men have created a *petite chamber* for me. Kimbrell fils leaves and returns minutes later with a small, round-topped table supported by three simply curved legs and a thin pedestal, all in the same gleaming pink wood.

"Merci!" I cry. *"Merci, messiers!"* The words simply flow out. Then to my further surprise, I do two things that will later shame me. I curtsy—to the workers. And I bring the featherbed—myself!—to the new bed and place it on the pale ropes strung into the beautiful wood.

Voilà! A room. I shall make a drawing for the wall. I shall ask Talon for additional candles and holder. It is all so exciting that I forget that Florentine, as a guest, needs attending, until he says, "Well, I shall report them, comte, even if you are disinclined, given your republican tendencies."

Outside, the two joiners carry Madame de Sevigny's harp somewhere. A comical sight—the gilded harp sailing through the day. I nearly laugh aloud. But then it is not so comical when it brings to mind how mobs looted our great houses in France. And how they probably have taken the Queen's own harp by now.

And perhaps the Queen herself.

Non! Let it not be, Our Lady. May she arrive here safely, and soon.

How fleeting, happiness. It wings away on a mere thought. Just moments earlier I was charmed by my *petite chamber*. The Latin phrase is so applicable: *Multum in parvo*. Much in little. But now I see it for what it is—next to nothing!

When Florentine finally leaves, I enter my new chamber and let tears fall. Maman parts the curtain and sits alongside me.

"Eugenie," she whispers, her arm holding me close to her. "*Ma chérie*. Enough, please. We must go to Madame de Sevigny this afternoon."

"I do not wish to go!"

"But we must. She will show us her new *maison*."

"What is there to see? It will look just like this one."

"Shall I tell you a story? About Versailles?"

"*Non.*"

I know all her stories by heart. The Presentation of Marie Antoinette to the People of Paris. The Ascension to the Throne. How Maman once Stepped on the Train of the Lady Ahead of Her in Procession. On and on they go, these stories—the masked balls, the witticisms, the intrigues, the triumphs. Maman loves retelling them because they transport her back to court life. I feel mean saying no. She is gently rubbing my forehead as if I were a little girl again, and ill.

"All right, Maman. One."

"I'm thinking of when you were invited to attend the *fête* for Marie-Thérèse at Le Petite Trianon. She was six and you, four, Eugenie. A white coach and four white horses took you there. Do you remember that June day? The strawberries? The lambs you played with, the Queen's special lambs? The sweet brown calves? You wore a watered silk gown, green, it had an amusing name, that color—"

"Frog green."

"*Oui!* Oh, Eugenie, you were so beautiful that day and so—"

"Happy."

"*Oui!* Happy. And you shall be again, Eugenie. It shall all be again."

"The peasants destroyed Le Petite Trianon. They took the animals and cut down its fruit trees. Monsieur Deschamps said so."

"That gardener should not talk so much, and you should not listen to his stories. They make you too sad."

"But they are true, Maman. He brought roots that he's planting even now, near the Queen's new house."

"Well, my stories are also true. And I do not make you weep. Now. I want to tell you something that may cheer you, *ma chérie.*"

I let my thoughts drift, for Maman seems about to embark upon another story of court life. But then she is saying, "Florentine adores you, and he is of such good family. I am thinking that we must arrange your marriage, Eugenie. You are exactly the Queen's age when she was married to the Dauphin. It will give us something to anticipate with joy—in addition to our Queen's arrival, of course. Is this not a wonderful idea? Then when we return to France, you shall have your own beautiful château, Eugenie, and—"

"Maman." The word hardly has breath behind it.

"He will inherit the title of comte, Eugenie. I had hoped for something higher for you, but . . ."

"*Non*, Maman!" Fear has found voice. I am shouting.

"Eugenie!"

"I am sorry, Maman, but not Florentine."

"Your father and I have discussed it and—"

"*Non!*"

I push away from her. My face is hot and must look scarlet. I care not!

"When you are calm, Eugenie, we shall discuss this matter."

Then I am alone in my *petite chamber*. "Sylvette," I whisper. "Where are you?"

After a while, she is curled alongside me as I lie there, shaking.

⸎ Hannah

Our baked loaves fill the air with sweetness.

In a happy turning, Madame Rouleau ordered Estelle, the youngest slave, to use our hearth to bake their bread. The one in the Rouleaux's cabin is too small for everything the family requires. Estelle has said—by gesture and a few words—that her mother is not well, and her master does not want any of them near, and that is the true reason.

'Tis no wonder they be ill, living in that hut of sticks, with winter nigh!

Well, Estelle doesn't look sick in the least, and she makes fine company. The work is cheerier and goes faster. Emmeline Cooper, Mary Worthington, Rachel Stalk, and the new hired girls are too busy with their own duties for the French to be any sort of company, even on First Day. So it is most good to have Estelle here, on these early darkening days.

And 'tis a lesson, too, how she has forgiven us for causing those whippings. I have yet to be able to forgive Mr. Rouleau.

After we carry out the last loaf to cool on the long board, Estelle suddenly curtsies to me and says, "*Merci, mademoiselle!*"

Because we have been laughing so much at little things— a tree full of crows, the baby chipmunk on the window ledge wanting our bread—I forget myself and take a few steps backward and bend my knees. It throws me off balance and I teeter like some rickety pole.

We laugh and repeat the fun. But then there is Mademoiselle de La Roque, coming across the uppermost crossroad. She has a clear view of our antics.

"Estelle!" I whisper. But Estelle is again curtsying and laughing. *"Non, non!"* I say. Estelle goes still. Mademoiselle La Roque passes in silence.

It will go harder on Estelle than on me. I shake my head in apology. Inside, I am trembling so, I drop the wooden rising bowl. But somehow it doesn't crack. A while later, when we are filling baskets with the bread, Estelle turns slowly and stares at me, her eyes widely open.

"Qu'est ce que?" I whisper. What is it?

She blinks, and then I see Mademoiselle de La Roque standing in our open doorway, with her dog. Its tail wags as the dog looks directly at me, awaiting another bone. I cannot move.

Estelle turns to her and curtsies. Mademoiselle gives her a hard look, but then regards the bread.

"What is it?" I whisper again in French. Estelle can tell me nothing. She has become a statue.

Mademoiselle sweeps one gloved hand through the air and points to the hearth's oven. Estelle stands there, not even blinking.

"Dost thou wish a loaf of bread?" I ask in poor French she does not seem to understand. So I take one of the loaves and offer it to her.

She steps backward, her eyes going round. Then she makes another dancelike motion with her hands.

"Estelle!" I say. *"Qu'est ce que!"*

Estelle gestures toward mademoiselle. *"Faim!"*

Fam? What is fam?

Mademoiselle pantomimes eating.

Hungry!

I quickly slice one of the loaves and spread butter upon the pieces. I offer mademoiselle one. The bread is still warm. But she takes another step backward, her eyes even larger. Estelle finally returns to life and has the good sense to motion her to the table. Then Estelle holds Father's armchair out for her and takes a plate from the cupboard, which she sets before her. I keep slicing and buttering bread. I know not what else to do.

Mademoiselle removes her gloves. *"Merci!"* she says in musical tones. The little dog sits close beside her, and she feeds it a piece of the bread.

I am tired from the day's work and go to sit down, but mademoiselle shouts *Non, non,* and quite a bit more in French. I look to Estelle. She is of no help, standing well away from the table, clasping her elbows and hunching her shoulders.

I remember the whippings, the hut. Anger shakes me up and down and every which way. I go to Estelle and lead her to the table. "Thou must sit," I say. Estelle at first allows herself to be led—she is used to following orders. But when we near the table, she balks like a scared lamb. Mademoiselle takes all this in and I know that we are going to be punished.

So be it, Hannah.

Since Estelle won't come to the table, I carry John's chair to her. But she will not sit, not even farther from the table. Mademoiselle stares at us. So does her little dog. I take our third chair and position it nearly in the center of the room and sit down alongside the empty chair Estelle is hanging onto.

Oh, Hannah, she will think thou art mad.

But mademoiselle only takes another piece of bread and quickly eats it.

"Délicieux!"

Estelle is shaking even while holding onto the chair back with both hands. Mademoiselle eats yet another piece of bread. My face feels numb. There's movement out on the road, a flash of color. Mr. La Roque, come looking for his daughter?

No. 'Tis the sour young Frenchman. I quickly look down, hoping he won't notice our open door, but he comes within three paces and stops. Mademoiselle does not see him; her back is to the door. I await the worst tongue-lashing yet, but he only turns away and keeps walking.

Was he looking for her? If so, why not address her? Is it because she is in our house?

Estelle quietly lets forth her breath. We await mademoiselle's next command, but she just looks at the loaf of bread on the table.

I go back to the table and cut several more slices and then butter each. I pour her a cup of black tea. Then I return to my chair in the center of the room and sit.

Finally she stands, shakes out her gown, and gathers her dog up into her arms. *"Merci,* Hannah Kimbrell," she says, walking out into sunlight.

Merci, Hannah Kimbrell. Merci, Hannah Kimbrell. Merci, Hannah . . .

The words won't leave.

Estelle places her hand over her heart to show me how frightened she was—and probably still is. But I'm only hearing that *Merci, Hannah Kimbrell.*

A chiming bell.

Tonight, as Father, John, and I reflect upon the day, I find myself thinking about Estelle. Except for our language and the color of our skin, I do not see where we are different. She knows how to make bread; I know how to make bread. She likes our mild sunshine; I like it. She laughs at amusing things, and so do I. She loves her family; I love my family. Only, I am free and she is a slave. Why? 'Tis neither just nor understandable.

And here's another puzzle. The Rouleau young ladies. Yesterday one of them curtsied to a noble lady, but the noble lady did not address her or curtsy in return. She just continued on her way with nary a glance at the Rouleau young lady. Had the noble lady looked, she would have seen a face all hurt and not-wanting-to cry. The Rouleau young lady will not talk to us, and not a one of the nobles will talk to *her*. What sense does this make? Naught. What way is this for people to live? Foolish and wasteful and sad, to my thought. A ruination of the day's joy. And since I seem bent upon puzzles this evening, here are yet others. What led Mademoiselle La Roque to write to me about the slaves being whipped? And why did she come to our house today?

Here. At our table. A French noble! A vision filling me not with fear but warmth.

Eugenie

"It was a mistake to even go near that place. Never do so again!"

"But Maman . . ."

"You are lonely. I understand. Soon, *chérie*, the Queen will be here. Marie Antoinette with Marie-Thérèse and Louis-Charles! Perhaps you and Madame Royale, the *princesse*, shall grow closer here. Imagine! And one day you may even have the great honor of serving as a lady of honor, as I myself did. Think of it! Marie Antoinette will come, and we must be ready to receive her. *La Grande Maison* will glow."

"Maman? What if the Queen scorns the house? It is not so grand, you know. Hardly a Versailles. It is merely . . . a large log *maison*."

Maman draws back her shoulders. She raises her chin. "Au contraire, *chérie*. For now, it is a symbol and shall stand for the thing itself until we are able to return—together. And until then, we shall have this!"

Holding a bit of her gown between two fingertips, Maman gracefully begins a minuet. She is so beautiful, she gives light to our *petite maison*. But then I gaze out our one window and see Kimbrell *fils* bringing wood to the Aversilles. In better clothing and finely made wig, he might be considered *élégant* by the most discerning of ladies. Educate him in the art of the bon mot, in dance, *boules*, cards, and the proper etiquette, of course, and he would fit in well at Versailles. His sanguine complexion speaks of good health and vigor. The eyes, of quick wit. But there he is instead, by some act of Providence, delivering firewood to French nobles improbably confined to this wilderness.

Through discreet inquiry I've learned that his Christian name is John. There was, I believe, an English king by that name.

"What are you looking at, Eugenie?"

"Nothing, Maman. The day."

"Come here, then. I must dress your hair. The Du Valliers visit this evening. I hardly know what to serve them. We must get another servant! And how shall we all fit in this room? *Mon Dieu!*"

"Maman? Why is rank necessary?"

"Rank? Our Lord Himself bestows power upon our kings and queens, and they upon us. It has always been thus."

"Our Lord . . . in his human form . . . He was a common man, was he not? His disciples, fishermen?"

"You have been talking with Americans!"

"*Non*, Maman. Just . . . thinking."

"Then you must stop. We have not come through all we have to simply throw away our titles now. Our very identities. We are who we are and must be, Eugenie. It is ordained. Surely you understand that."

"I . . . do, Maman."

"*Bon.* Now. What shall you wear this evening, for the Du Valliers?"

"Anything you wish."

"Eugenie! Show some enthusiasm, please."

"Maman? I miss my Henriette. Do you think she is . . . still alive?"

"She is still alive, Eugenie. Bernard is caring for her."

"Do you think so? Really think so?"

Maman sighs. "You must wear your yellow gown tonight. It is festive. Hopeful."

"Henriette looked so sad, Maman, when I ran to the stable for the last time."

"And endangered all of us. You will wear your necklace tonight, Eugenie. Grand-mere's diamonds may divert attention from the cuisine."

"I wish . . ."

"What do you wish, *ma chérie?*"

"That I might ride one of those horses. Out there."

Maman looks through the window. "They are but work horses."

"*Oui,* yet beautiful."

"You are becoming as troublesome as your father. We must take care or the Du Valliers may think better of an alliance with our family. Florentine saw you with a servant and a slave today. I pray he will not relay this to his parents, but no doubt he will."

"No doubt."

These words of Maman's give me an idea.

I look out the window yet again. Kimbrell *fils* is nearly finished unloading the wagon. Do I imagine that he glances this way from time to time?

"Eugenie. Come! Your hair!"

"*Oui,* Maman. *Oui.*"

Hannah

Snow blurs the mountain across the river. It rushes down in fat bundles of flakes. Yesterday was a clear cold, with morning frost thick as snow, and today true snow, with wind from the northwest cutting across the settlement. Within this wind fly more geese. They like to ride the northwest winds. It all feels like the first stroke of winter.

The clothing won't dry well today. How I wish Father and John had time to finish the drying shed.

And here comes Mademoiselle de La Roque, with Sylvette. Yesterday she was here to watch a small flotilla arriving with supplies, but no French people. She turned away after throwing a few sticks for Sylvette.

I begin taking down the linens. Father and John will not like all the lines strung in our cabin, but maybe this'll hurry them along with the shed.

Mademoiselle holds a blue parasol. Sylvette wears a blue jacket. 'Tis a sight. A parasol in the snow. A dog in a jacket! The jacket is but a piece of cloth tied around with ribbons and bows. I smile as I search my pockets—and yes!—find a bone wrapped in paper. But mademoiselle stands over by herself, and I don't know whether I should go any closer.

It is the dog who makes the decision. She runs to me and dances on her small hind legs. Then mademoiselle comes a bit closer. Her eyes are red, and her face a blotchy pink. She has been crying. 'Tis hard to see her waiting in hope when there may be no other flotillas until spring. Supplies might come by pack train, but the river is becoming too danger-ous, now, for boats. And soon it will be icebound. I do not like to think of her here every day, looking downriver for something that won't be coming.

It makes me want to learn, really learn, her language. Because if I knew French, I could tell her how I miss my family, too. Mother and Suzanne and Grace and Richard. I could say how I don't feel like myself because so much is missing. And not being on our farm, that too.

But look! She has not walked away. *Courage, Hannah!* I will say just one word to her. A person ought not be fined too much for just one word.

"Maman." I point downriver.

She turns to me. Her little mouth curves downward, wanting to scold.

"Ma famille," I continue.

She looks downriver. *"Votre famille?"*

"Oui."

"Ah! *Famille!*"

She lifts the dog and holds her close to her rust-red cloak.

"Sylvette," I say, and dare to extend my hand to her. Mademoiselle steps away from me. Unlike her mistress, the dog is such a friendly little creature. She wriggles and seems to be smiling as she strains toward me. Her white fur is all curls and looks to be very soft, like clumped milkweed seeds. Her nose is black, as are her eyes. Her ears are white mittens I long to touch. Just once! I imagine silk must feel somewhat this way.

I show mademoiselle the bone. Sylvette squirms, and

mademoiselle allows her to leap down. Then she nods at me, and I give Sylvette the bone.

I wish I could ask whether the little dog has come all the way from France or if mademoiselle got her here in America. Other questions come. Where had her home been, in France? And what is the countryside like? Are there farms such as ours? What crops are grown? How large are the towns? Are they beautiful? Do all people in France have musical instruments such as the one in her cabin? Was she happy in France, before the troubles there?

I wonder if she has any questions to ask of me.

But she only looks over her shoulder every so often while Sylvette gnaws on the bone. Finally she urges the little dog to come with her, and Sylvette does, carrying the bone.

I remember the bean soup simmering on our hearth. And my corn bread. "Mademoiselle, *attendez!*" I call. "Wait!"

She turns. I gesture toward our cabin at the end of the clearing. *"Mangez?"*

"Je regrette."

She is sorry! I want to ask why but am too frightened to say anything more.

Snow whitens her cloak and feathered hat. Walking away, she looks like a small old woman uncertain of every step.

Inside me there is something very like a cut. Perhaps she is not allowed to come to our cabin. Perhaps she does not want to, ever again.

On the way back, I circle past Estelle's hut and hide a packet of dried apples, dried venison, and a candle in a patch of yellowing fern. 'Tis our usual spot. Estelle's hut looks the same, merely a heap of pine boughs woven into a lattice of poles. But at least we have been able to smuggle them food as well as some oiled cloth for walls and the earthen floor. And Alain, Estelle's brother, has made them pallets for beds. He used scraps of wood the joiners secretly put aside for him. It is saddening to think of him out in the middle of the night, searching for these bits of wood, with no other light than that of the moon. All the nobles and all the workers, including the French ones, have cabins now. Only the slaves do not. Seeing their hut these days always makes me worry about the approaching winter. Mr. Rouleau may not know how cold it can get here. When he does, he might relent.

Well, at least we have made them boots, John and I. And that is to the good.

Eugenie ☙

Sylvette looks dressed for a ball, with her white jacket tied around with pink, blue, and yellow ribbons. I hold her blue-ribbon leash as we walk to the river. It is good to be walking unfettered by Florentine's presence. Good not to have to think of witty rejoinders. And on a day of sunlight and near warmth! Yesterday's snow has melted, and the river rushes on, brown and high, yet today's sunlight dresses it with light, and all seems more hopeful.

But every so often I look over my shoulder and to either side for wild animals, though I cannot believe that they would just charge into our clearing. There is too much noise from the carpentry, the joiners working on new *maisons*—another hopeful sign—and on *La Grande Maison*, too.

I remove my gloves and find a stick to throw for Sylvette. For this I must release the blue ribbon. It always makes me worry that she might just rush off into the woods, on the scent of something. And then that will be the end of her.

"Sylvette, stay close now, *ma petite*. Here is your stick."

I toss it nearby and she runs, in her ribbons and jacket—a comical sight. I toss the stick again and again. The third time she catches it in midair, but lets it fall from her mouth. Then she begins barking.

I turn, fearing Florentine's presence. But it is the petty despot Rouleau, with the slave girl Estelle. They are farther along the landing and walking down to the water. She carries something while he loudly berates her. "Who do you think you are, accepting such gifts? I have told you before. You are to accept nothing from those people! They are meddlers. They cause only trouble. While you—you have gotten sly, haven't you? Hiding things from us. Secretive! And who knows? Even plotting, maybe!"

"*Non*, monsieur, we—"

"Dare not contradict me!"

Sylvette is shivering and growling as I carry her up the landing, away from them. Still Rouleau has not seen us. At the top of the landing I look back. Rouleau and the girl are at the water's edge. He has her throw something into the water and then shouts that she hasn't thrown it far enough. Sylvette squirms to be free. She longs to chase whatever it is. I hold her tightly.

Rouleau takes something else from the girl and heaves it into the center of the rapid river. It immediately sinks. She hands him another object. He throws it and it, too, sinks. The next time something arcs over the river, I shade my eyes and look carefully. A boot! They are throwing boots into the water. Why in heaven's name are they doing that? Four have gone in. Then another, another, and finally still two others. Then the arm that has been heaving the boots out over the water flies toward the girl, striking her on the head. She falls to one knee on the stones. He raises his arm again.

"Monsieur Rouleau," I call, as I move closer.

He turns and, seeing us, bows. "Ah, my lady! I am merely teaching my servant an important lesson. Allow me to proceed, if you please."

"And what lesson might that be, Monsieur Rouleau?"

"One in obedience. You would agree, would you not, that such lessons are necessary for our servants. Otherwise"—his shoulders lift and fall—"we have anarchy and rebellion and even revolution."

"How is this girl rebelling?"

"By accepting what I ordered her not to accept."

"And what might that be?"

"Gifts—from the Americans. The free-thinking Americans."

"What, exactly, have they given her?"

"Boots, my lady, when I forbade it."

"Boots! Can they not use boots? Are boots not useful in their work for you?"

"Be that as it may, I have forbidden it, and I am their master. Not the Americans. My slaves must not have divided loyalties."

"Which Americans in particular have given your slaves boots?"

"The Kimbrells, mademoiselle."

"The ones who attempted to build them a *maison?*"

"Indeed, the very ones."

"And why do you not wish them to have a house?"

"Pardon me, but it is not for me to fully explain my reasoning to you, mademoiselle. Perhaps you might ask your father for enlightenment. Or the marquis. Now, if you will excuse me."

Roughly, he pulls the girl away from the river. She has nothing at all on her feet!

In this cold. In the mud.

"Monsieur Rouleau! You are a cruel man. And as stupid as those peasants who tore up the gardens at Le Petit Trianon out of spite."

He glowers but is clever enough not to reply.

"Also, you have ruined my morning!"

"Is something wrong, Eugenie?" Maman asks at our dinner.

There is rye bread and cheese on my plate, and a dish of applesauce on the side. There is even a spice cake at the center of our table. I have been looking at all this food for some time but cannot eat.

"Eugenie!" Maman says. "The cheese is decent, as is the bread. Our servant has not managed to ruin these, at least. Are you becoming ill, my daughter?"

"Papa, Maman—I believe I now understand something about freedom."

"And what is that?" Papa says.

"I think . . . it is a state of being in which we can better our situation. We have the right, at least, to do so if we choose. The opposite is . . . slavery. If one is a slave, then one has no such right or power. One cannot better one's situation at all."

"Are there Americans here," Maman asks, "who speak such good French?"

"I have talked with no one! It is what I have seen for myself."

When I finish telling them about Rouleau and the boots, Papa strikes the table. He has not done so since we left France. "The man is a tyrant! I must speak to Talon."

"He will simply call you a republican."

"He may call me what he wishes, but we should not tolerate such behavior here, in our settlement. The man is getting his revenge for having been burnt out. He is taking out his anger on his few loyal slaves, slaves who helped put out the fires on his plantation! Rouleau himself tells the story with satisfaction. His behavior violates human decency. I am going to speak with him this night."

"Who? Not Rouleau?"

"Talon."

"There was not supposed to be strife here," Maman says.

"What is supposed to be and what *is* seldom conjoin, I am afraid."

When he leaves, Maman says, "I wish you would just remain inside, Eugenie. Play the harpsichord. Read. Why must you be out so much?"

"Sylvette needs her walk, and I, too, or I shall forget how."

"Then go with Florentine. He at least can . . . protect you."

"Oh, Maman, I would probably be the one to protect him!"

"Are you perhaps seeing what you tell yourself to see?"

"I do not think so, Maman."

"*Oui,* I believe you are. Now. Ready yourself. The Du Valliers visit us this evening."

"Oh, Maman. He is so boring. Besides, he likes only himself."

"Eugenie. I beg you. At least give him an opportunity to prove himself."

A sad day, after its good start. But that is how it often is, I'm learning. Starting well, ending badly. Or starting badly and ending well. Like weather.

✆ Hannah

"Hannah Kimbrell, I require you to make three fine cakes. These may be of the same variety but must be exceptional. I have been told that you are the best baker in this settlement, so, mademoiselle, I am obliged to compromise and bow to your superior abilities even though you refuse to return the courtesy." Mr. Talon bows, which causes heat to rush to my face. "The *fête* is in honor of our Queen's birthday. We celebrate it three weeks late for the simple reason that we were not here on November 2, but now here we are! Rachel Stalk will come for the cakes. You are not to go near the nobles and cause offense. I also require you to make your venison stew. Others will come for it."

As he turns away, his cloak creates a breeze.

In our large storeroom I make an assessment. Apples. Cinnamon. Mace. Pepper. Salt. Cornstarch. Arrowroot. Smyrna raisins. Black walnuts. Chestnuts. Cornmeal. Wheat flour. Maple syrup. Mushrooms. Potatoes. Lard. Dried beans of several sorts. Onions. Carrots and turnips in sand. Smoked fish, smoked venison, and ham. Many of these supplies have come from Mr. Talon, like the wheat and spices, the cornmeal and lard and raisins, so that I can cook for the workers and the Aversilles. The maple syrup is our own, and the potatoes, beans, turnips, and carrots, these coming from the garden we planted here last spring. The dried fish and venison, too, our own. The walnuts and mushrooms as well. We keep an account of all we use for ourselves and for the others. Each month Mr. Talon asks for these accounts so we can settle up. I do like not doing sums, but 'tis at least good practice.

I pack a basket for a little meal and walk into the woods behind our cabin and up the hill a ways, passing the springhouse Father and John built. It sits atop the bubbling spring that gives us our fresh water. Here we keep our milk and eggs and the butter I make weekly.

Apple cake, I decide, with black walnuts, cinnamon, and ground chestnut meal. Thick cream poured over the top. Or, whisked into frothy peaks.

I hurry farther up the hill toward the grove of black walnut trees. There's been wind enough to blow even the trees themselves down. John will be yodeling in protest when he learns that he is "required" to shell more black walnuts. So many more! They are the hardest nut of all to shell. John has to smash them between flat river stones. The shells we use as kindling, but they are sharp enough, surely, for use as tools of some kind.

Right off, I see jugfuls and begin to pick. They are everywhere amid the fallen leaves. I am making such a ruckus, I only faintly hear a crackling somewhere nearby. Then I know, even before I look up. My heart knows. It fairly stops beating and then pounds on in my ears.

A mountain lion. She has dropped down not twenty feet away. Tawny as the leaves, and with the sun and shade playing over her fur, she is almost invisible.

To run will mean death. Kneeling, I keep very still, the basket before me.

"Go," I say quietly.

Her long tail twitches a little and flicks from side to side a bit. Her eyes do not leave me as she steps slowly forward, each large paw crunching leaves. Her whiskers glint in the sun like long silver needles.

"*Go away,* Mistress Lion."

She takes another step forward and pauses, her tail still flicking, her head quite still. At the tip of each ear fur stands up in tiny points of light.

Hardly moving myself, I reach into the basket and bring out the dried fish. Even this much movement may cause her to spring forward.

Father, John, Mother—farewell. I have loved thee much. And Grace, Suzanne, Richard.

"If thou shall not leave, have this!"

Her mouth opens as she sniffs the air. Quickly, I toss the fish. It lands near her forelegs, and she lowers her head to it. When she settles on her haunches and begins tearing at it, I grab up my basket and run.

Down, down past the springhouse. Down past the oaks and into our cabin.

Inside, I am shaking hard as any forest of leaves. Quite awhile later I notice all the black walnuts, still in the basket.

I look up at the Kentucky rifle above our mantle.

But she has spared my life, and so I shall spare hers—by saying nothing.

"Take much care with this, Rachel. Thou knowest not what all has gone into the making of it. And there be two others to carry over as well."

With small unsteady hands, Rachel takes the large platter. I watch that she doesn't stumble and fall with it. Her doing so would hurt me more than the nobles' not knowing who made it.

'Tis true, how much does go into the making of a thing. Thought and feeling and effort and sometimes danger, too. And so the thing finally becomes all of that, and is good.

After feeding our animals, John and I stand outside awhile, listening to music coming from the marquis's cabin near the center of the clearing. 'Tis wondrous, truly! Like rushing water. Or the swirl of stars at night.

"Dost thou think they be dancing?" John asks.

"There may not be enough room for dancing."

"Dost thou think it be a hard thing to learn?"

"Dancing? I think thou, John, do harder things every day."

"I believe not."

"John, 'tis mere amusement."

"Aye."

"Dost thou wish to dance?"

"Nay."

"It is for those who, unlike us, have little else to occupy them."

"Aye."

"Imagine, though, being able to make such music! That must take much time to learn."

His arms hang at his sides. He stares in the direction of the cabin. "Dost thou think she is there, Hannah?"

"Who, John?"

"Mademoiselle de La Roque."

"She may well be."

"You say she talks to thee now, sometimes?"

I begin to understand. "Ah, John," I say finally. "Thou art a foolish boy if thou thinks—"

"I think nothing!" Quick, he turns and enters our cabin. I follow him and offer apology for calling him foolish.

"Nay," he says, "thou art right, Hannah."

I say nothing further, for John's eyes shy from mine.

Father tells us how the marquis devised a clever plan— the French families again drew lots to see when their time of calling upon Mr. Talon might be. They liked this idea, Father says. They are used to games of chance. "For them 'tis like the spices in your cake, Hannah."

It is near eleven when Rachel returns with our platter, plates, and stewpot, everything clean. "I thank thee, Rachel."

"Oh, your cakes, Hannah, they be greatly received. The French want to know who made them! Talon tells them you, Hannah! At least he be honest, no? He says to tell you if only you might curtsy half so well, you could name your price with any of the French families. Imagine! Ye'd be rich, Hannah, an' I wouldn't need t'work so hard. They want so much all the time, I can noways keep up. An' they always complain no matter how good I go an' do a thing."

"Rachel, 'tis a foolish custom. To curtsy. But more, 'tis wrong."

"Do you set yourself above them, then?"

"Nay. They set themselves above us."

"My father says that you Quakers be too big for yer britches, Hannah Kimbrell, and goin' for a fall. All you Kimbrells."

Surely we do not set ourselves above them, I want to say. We only believe in equality. But to say so now would not be seemly, would take us too near argument. So I say naught. Still, 'tis something to ponder, the question of pride.

"Ah, but Hannah, ye shoulda seen 'em in their finery. Never such a sight will I pro'ly see ever again. Earrings, Hannah, that match the necklaces, bracelets, and brooches. And gowns so fanciful and shinylike you'd think angels were a'wearin' 'em."

While Rachel yarns on, I am wondering about pride. Do we think we're better? Or do we feel lower and yet think we're better because we have courage and are proud of it?

"Ye shoulda seen the La Roque girl, Hannah. She wore a necklace that fair blinded me. Icy stones and blue ones, the blue ones so blue. What might they be, Hannah, do ye know?"

"I know not, surely. Bits of colored glass perhaps. Or stone."

"Well, I never saw the like. And the young gentleman with her, he never left her side!"

"The one who frowns so much?"

"Aye. The very one. Only he weren't, tonight."

Poor John, I think.

"That necklace—'tis but pieces of earth, Rachel. Nothing more. Why, we could make necklaces of river stones if we had a mind to. Polish those to glittering, but to what good, such vanity?"

"What did ye say, Hannah?"

"It be simple vanity."

Rachel Stalk sighs. "Aye. But a pretty vanity all the same. Oh! I be remembering. She said to give you this."

A pink satin ribbon! Long as one of Sylvette's leashes.

"She musta liked yer cake."

Thoughts spin me over head and ears. A gift? From her?

"Ye ain't gonna wear it, are ye?"

"No, Rachel." I see it against my dark braid, a flower there.

"Then might I have it? I'd like wearin' it, an' no rule 'gainst it for me."

Inside, I find my scissors and snip it in half, though it pains me to do so.

"I thank ye, Hannah! Ye be a good person though I don't see why ye couldna give it all, fer all yer talk about vanities."

I give her the other half. "For your braids, Rachel." Then I turn away before she can see my eyes filling. "Good night!"

1793

Decembre / December

Eugenie ❧

With feverish intensity, Maman says, "I must live to see my Queen."

"Oh, you shall, Maman! But if so, you must eat something." I offer, once again, the porridge. "Our new servant made this, Maman. Not Rachel Stalk. Have some, *s'il te plaît!*"

"*Non!* Its smell makes me ill." As if to prove her words, poor Maman heaves into the basin Papa holds for her.

"That you should see me this way! *Mon Dieu.*"

The stench of the basin and the chamber pots is so thick and terrible, I grow light-headed. In my room, I lie down while everything whirls about and the room darkens. Closing my eyes does not help. There is still the smell, and the sensation of falling headlong down some chute.

"Call Annette," Maman is saying. "Call Annette, I say!"

"Charlotte," Papa says to Maman. "Charlotte, my dear."

"Isabel, then! Call them both, and summon Monsieur Robarge. Tell him that I have been poisoned. Does Sevigny want my position so badly?"

Maman is delirious. I fear she will die now, as delirious people often do.

"Eugenie," Papa says. "You must stop crying. It helps nothing. In fact, the opposite!"

His tone scares me into silence. Never before has he been this sharp with me. Then he says to Maman, "Ah! Monsieur

Robarge has just now arrived. We summoned him, and now he will care for you himself."

I hold Sylvette while Papa does his best to bathe Maman and change the linens. Icy air blows into our *maison* from our one window. Papa has hooked up the flap and the piece of tapestry so fresh air might enter and clear away the stench of sickness. Yet it is still so strong. And it, too, tells me that Maman will die. The river is frozen, and no boats shall come. No post riders can get through the high snow in the forest, and surely no physician. Why has not Talon foreseen such a thing? Because he is a proud, ignorant man.

Has Mary's cooking poisoned Maman? There is no jaundice, just the fever's flush. Surely even I could cook better than Mary Worthington and Rachel Stalk! Oh, what value to be good at cards or *boules* or the *quadrille* and *polonaise* and *allemande* but not know how to properly prepare food? How foolish to assume that there will always and forever be someone to do this for us, and do it well. I do not even know how to roast garlic.

Yet could I not learn?

Oui! Somehow I shall—for Maman, Papa, Sylvette, and myself. Living one's life as a helpless child is *absurde.*

A knock at our door!

No one has come to visit of late, everyone having heard of Maman's illness. Not even Florentine's mother so that she might gossip about us. I imagine a physician, summoned by Talon. But it is only our *abbé.* "Enter, please," Papa says, holding open the door to the cold. I know he wants to quickly shut it.

"Oh, no, thank you. I shall bless your dear wife from here." He sprinkles the room with his pine branch and departs, quite nimbly. He has lost nearly half his bulk, thanks to Rachel Stalk's fine cooking.

"So much for *le courage*," Papa says, shutting the door and barring it.

It is true. Our countrymen and women have been shunning us. Yesterday when I went out with Sylvette, Florentine's mother called from her *maison* window, "It is too cold to be out, mademoiselle! Go back inside!"

Go inside. Not come inside. Any illness, here, becomes the anteroom of death, it seems. Well, then, so let us die! Release us into the next life, surely better than this.

The thought shocks me. I do not wish to die, do I? Nor do I wish Maman to die. Nor Papa. And the thought of leaving Sylvette on her own, here, horrifies me.

I part the curtains and see Papa pacing in a small circle in front of the hearth while Maman moans and shivers, her face crimson. A bowl of melting snow is on the floor by her bed. I take the cloth from her brow, dip it in the ice water, wring it out, and put it back on her brow. Her skin is so hot and dry, like burning sand. Then I go to Papa and whisper two words. Papa stares at me a moment, his eyes a terrible red, but his face pale.

My Lord, please do not let him be ill, too.

Papa nods and in the next minute I am putting on my redingote.

Talon's team of Belgian horses and the v-shaped plow have not yet cleared the avenues. For a time I can follow Abbé La Barre's boot prints, but then soon must make my own. My feet sink in snow up to the knees, and I must hold my redingote and gown above the drifts as I walk—too slowly!— toward the cabin at the far end of the clearing.

It appears impossibly far away. So I think, instead, of the Grand Ballroom at Versailles, and flouncing over its gleaming floor in a polka, the music and every face *brillant,* and my body weightless as a bird's. But then I find myself tipping forward into a drift too high to climb. I am so tired I wish only to lie there and sleep.

Non! Rise, rise, Eugenie! You shall not die like some fallen bird in a snowdrift! Get up! Everyone needs you. Maman. Papa. Sylvette. You must get up. Now.

I fight against the powder, but the American snow has its own strength. And yet I am able to right myself and push forward. The *maison* grows larger, and soon there are fewer drifts. And then, finally, a swept-clear yard over which new flakes sparkle. I climb down into it, and then the door opens upon warmth and light, and Hannah is removing my shoes and placing my wet feet in a pan of warm water and my hands in another.

"Maman," I say. I keep repeating the word. Hannah nods.

Soon we are both trudging through the snow, my feet now in a pair of heavy wool stockings and American boots, and Hannah carrying a stewpot and basket of medicines and herbs.

Papa helps me back inside and urges Hannah to enter quickly, for the day is a frigid river flooding in around us. Maman opens her eyes, sees Hannah, and moans the word *non* several times. I go to her and whisper, "We have medicines for you, Maman." Lavender spots whirl before my eyes. I have to sit and lower my head.

Papa helps Maman sit up, and Hannah kneels on the floorboards and offers Maman a spoonful of broth. Maman closes her eyes.

"Do this for us if not yourself," Papa urges.

After a while Hannah stands. I fear she might leave, with her wondrous food and herbs. But she says, in her quiet manner, "Madame de La Roque."

Maman opens her eyes.

With both hands, Hannah raises her gown a bit, bows her head and takes one tottering step backward, all the while sinking low in—*mirabile dictu!*—a curtsy. She repeats the movement twice.

No one speaks for several moments. Then Maman says, *"Merci,"* and raises her handkerchief to each eye. Soon after, she begins swallowing the broth.

While I help Maman, Hannah takes the basin and chamber pots outside. When she returns, she cleans the floor around the bed and bundles up the soiled linens. She scalds her hands clean with hot water and sets our table.

We all feel somewhat better after Hannah's broth and sweet tea. Maman lies there sipping it, and although she shivers at times, she is at least more coherent now.

"Live, Maman," I tell her. "Our Queen is coming and we shall walk in the garden with her, the garden at *La Grande Maison.* There will be lilacs and roses and great tall irises. Monsieur Deschamps—do you remember the gardener?— well, he promises this! Remember how he told us that his flowers shall tame this wild air with their perfume? And so they shall, Maman! And we will dance again, and these flowers shall decorate our ballroom!"

She takes my hand and holds it a long while. In France I did not feel this close to her. Nor was I aware of any lack within myself, as I am here. But at least I know more, now, about weather, wind direction, the great cloudscapes, their array of colors and shapes and the way the light transforms them. I vow that when the promised shops open here in the spring, I shall buy some paints and canvas, if such luxuries are to be had. I shall paint these magnificent clouds. I shall paint Sylvette on the riverbank. I shall paint Maman and Papa, for Maman shall live. And I shall paint Hannah, too, and the gardens at *La Grande Maison,* for there *shall* be lilacs and laburnum, and fleur-de-lis, and our Queen shall walk there, in the garden, and Maman and I with her.

Sitting by the hearth while Maman sleeps, I recall how she taught me to curtsy. There are so many rules about how to hold one's gown and lower one's head and step backward in such a way, the gesture meant to be a butterfly's perfect flutter. But my little feet tangled, and I tumbled over and had to fight my way out of the snare of crinolines. I laughed and Maman with me. I could not know then that it would take months of practice to be able to do it even passably well, and years to perfect in all its variations. I wonder if Hannah will continue to curtsy for Maman. She did not curtsy to me when I half-fell into her *maison.* And, strangely, it did not seem a slight. In truth I did not think of it at all.

Maman could not sacrifice her pride but Hannah did. This fact holds forth no hope that Maman's attitude will ever ease. I can dream all I wish about learning how to make bread, but Maman will never allow it.

Later, after Hannah returns for the dishes and her pots, she curtsies first—to me! in her clumsy manner. I find myself smiling.

"Like this," I whisper in French, and then attempt to correct at least one awkwardness in the combination of them.

Valiantly, the girl tries to imitate me. *"Bon!"* I say, though it wasn't very good at all. Then Hannah steps out into the cold night, the pots and dishes rattling like a tinker's wagon.

Waking, Maman asks for water. I bring it to her and feel her forehead. It is not so hot or dry as before. In fact, there is moisture at her hairline and lips and a sheen to her face. "Maman! Hannah's tea has broken your fever. And she has curtsied! Can we have her back? As our servant?"

"The curtsy does not make her any different. She still possesses . . . revolutionary ideas. Do not dishonor us. The Du Valliers will never agree to an alliance."

Maman's voice rasps. I give her more water. "If I do not speak with her, can she at least be our cook? Or—could I speak with her in our *maison?* Just here, Maman? No one will see. No one will know! Oh, allow it, please."

We await her decision.

It comes, finally. "You must maintain dignity and rank."

"Oui, Maman. But as for her cooking, can we not at least have that as well as our dignity and rank?"

"But nothing more. Do not speak with her other than to give an order."

After Maman falls asleep, Papa and I each have a cup of tea and quietly express our relief about Maman. Although we are both fatigued, neither of us, it seems, wants to let go of this peaceful respite in favor of sleep. "What is that, Papa?" I ask, noticing the piece of paper next to our candle in its pewter holder.

"Oh, merely something I have been trying to understand."

"Is it important?"

He smiles with weariness. "To many people, yes, it is. Most important."

Papa goes on to explain that it is a French translation of the Americans' Declaration of Independence. "I found it in Philadelphia. See these names at the bottom? Traitors all, according to the English king."

"But France came to their aid. Why, Papa?"

"No doubt because it was beginning to appear that the Americans might win, against our old enemy."

"Yet they were rebels, the Americans."

"It does seem contradictory. Certainly a paradox—our nobles and navy supporting the American rebels. Here is something else I've been trying to understand. It says that some truths are self-evident. Do you know what that means?"

"That we should understand them right away? Without much thought?"

"Exactly. And what is supposedly self-evident? That men are created equal. That they have rights given them by our Creator. That if someone in authority violates these rights, then . . . it is allowable to overthrow him . . . or her. To me, Eugenie, all this has not been self-evident."

"Papa, did the Kimbrells get their idea of equality from this Declaration?"

"Possibly. Equality. The rebels in France call for that. *Liberté, equalité, fraternité!*"

"So the French rebels took this idea from the Americans! No wonder Maman worries."

"In fact, *chérie,* some of our own philosophers have put forth these ideas first. What I have been thinking, however, is that it was not self-evident to me because . . ." Papa rubs his eyes, and then the sore-looking place underneath each. "I refused to even allow the thought. Until now."

"When the Queen comes, will you still think about such things?"

"I believe . . . yes. I will."

I cannot sleep. My thoughts are a flock of birds trying to settle but then veering upward again and again. *Egualité!* Self-evident . . .

"Never mind, Sylvette," I whisper. "When the Queen comes, all will be as before. And Maman will live. And even the wind shall stop this mad shrieking."

Finally, sleep, but with it comes the dream. I hear shouting. See smoke. The fire surrounding Annette. I cry out but make no sound. The air is bright with fire, and Maman and Papa are gone.

My chest hurts when I open my eyes.

Our *maison* seems quite cold. Parting my curtain, I see that our hearth fire is merely a pile of glowing embers. It must not be allowed to go out! I get up and take one of the logs near the hearth—surprisingly heavy—and drop it upon the embers, causing a crackle of sparks. I take another and drop it alongside the first. Tendrils of smoke rise and a moment later, shoots of flame spring up.

Mon Dieu. Have I myself built up the fire?

Pride nudges away fear. I have! I, Eugenie Annette Marie de La Roque, have done something useful!

Tonight it means life, Sylvette. Warmth. Light. Life.

Hannah

I enter with the cider and curtsy to each of them. Madame de La Roque nods. Mademoiselle blushes and points to the hearth where a good fire burns. She points to herself.

Has she herself built up the fire? Often Mr. La Roque does, but has she, this time? I smile at her. She returns the smile. She has, I think. But why are they being so quiet? Why do they not speak to me? I have been learning many French words and so wish to use them. At least try! And what is different about Mademoiselle de La Roque today?

Oh! 'Tis her hair! White as on the day she came through the snow to our cabin.

I warm the cider at their fire while mademoiselle arranges her mother's hair in high swirls and rolls. She pins switches into the hair—they put me in mind of squirrels' tails. Then she blends the tails in with the other hair. Soon Madame La Roque's hair is a high loaf of brown bread. Mademoiselle de La Roque takes something from a small tin and dabs it over the rolls and curls. Finally she upends a canister, and a dusting of powder falls onto the mass, but not quite changing the brown to white. Madame de La Roque's hair now looks like a snowshoe hare just coming into winter.

Mademoiselle turns and dangles one of the switches before me. She is smiling but still says nothing. What does she want? Is she not allowed to speak to me?

I suspect this must be the reason for her silence. Again she dangles a brown switch and points to my hair.

"*Non, non,* mademoiselle, *s'il vous plaît!*"

"Eugenie! *Arretez!*" Madame de La Roque says as mademoiselle comes near.

Mademoiselle dangles the switch for Sylvette, instead. Sylvette leaps for it, and they play awhile, but mademoiselle looks sad. So I undo my braid and quickly pile up my hair, then hold it in its "cloud." This makes mademoiselle smile, but her mother repeats the word *arretez* several times and motions for me to leave.

I do, after curtsying to each of them again.

"Father," I say during our evening meal. "I must tell thee, for it weighs upon my heart. I have been curtsying to the La Roque family."

John looks up from his plate. Father, too. Both appear startled as raccoons.

"Forgive me for disobeying thee. Madame was so ill." I go on to tell them how Mademoiselle de La Roque came asking for help, but how her mother refused my broth and tea.

"She is now well?"

"She is."

"Yet thou continue to curtsy?"

"They shall send me away, otherwise."

"And thou dost not wish to be sent elsewhere to work?"

"No, Father. I much like . . . mademoiselle and her little dog. I do not feel that I am . . . less, Father, because of the curtsy. I only wish them to be well. And not have to have young Rachel Stalk's cooking. Or Mary's. Not that they are . . . without skill."

Father smiles at that.

"Dost thou curtsy to the Aversilles as well, or anyone else?"

"No, Father. Madame d'Aversille keeps a tally. Sometimes she strikes through it when pleased by what I do. Other noble ladies keep tallies, too. But the marquis so far has not forbidden me to cook for the La Roques or the Aversilles."

"It may be that Philippe de La Roque has talked to him."

"Has he ever required thou and John to bow, Father?"

"Nay. And few noble gentlemen come near our work, except for the one who walks about so much, Mr. Sevigny. But he seems addled most of the time."

"Dost thou even know how to curtsy, Hannah?" John asks.

"Mademoiselle has been trying to teach me."

I see Father's sad look and apologize again.

"Daughter, dost thou feel that they are greater than thou?"

"No, Father."

"Then 'tis a means to an end."

"Aye." I am further dismayed, thinking how Father taught us that the end never justifies the means.

"And so not a little tinged with hypocrisy."

I draw in a long breath. "I knew not what else to do, Father, and mademoiselle has become more friendly of late. She even . . . speaks to me."

"As well she should. Daughter, decide in thy heart what is best. Only . . ." Again Father regards me sadly. "Do not allow it to confuse thee."

"Father, I do wonder. They have been to many places in our world. They read much. They play musical instruments."

"And thou?"

"I read the Bible. Sometimes *Poor Richard's Almanac*. I cook. I bake. I tend to animals. I wash clothes."

"Dost Madame de La Roque know how to make butter?"

"No, Father."

"Can she milk a cow?"

I laugh.

"Or shear a sheep and spin wool?"

"It would be a wondrous sight, indeed."

"Aye. So you see, our talents may be different, yet as people we are equal. 'Tis a simple matter, truly, yet apt to be confused by outward things. The way one dresses or speaks. What one does to earn one's bread. It seems a human weakness, wanting to put value where none exists."

"Why is it that Mr. La Roque seems so different than the others?"

"Well, he has seen much, in France, these past months."

"But the others must have seen many of the same things."

"Aye, but seeing and understanding do not always go hand in hand. Nor understanding and our actions."

"As with me."

"But thy motivation is selfless, and that's to the good."

"Shall I stop, Father, and let them just . . . be? On their own?"

"Follow thy heart, Hannah."

"I like not being . . . false."

"Then do not curtsy."

These words make me triste, which means *sad* in French.

"John," Father says, "thou art quiet tonight."

"A bit weary."

Aye, I think. And confused of heart, too.

"Father," I say, "here's another matter. Those slaves."

"It troubles me as well. I have been trying to puzzle through it."

John and I wait, but Father says no more until I clear the table. Then he says, "Let us have our evening reflection."

My thoughts are leaves swirling. And my feelings. Curtsy or not? Will we be able to help the slaves? Fit belief to action there?

Decidedly, I want to. That thought is the brightest leaf of all.

Mayhap 'tis well we have come here after all. 'Tis no small thing to do some good.

In the lean-to washhouse, I notice how Estelle's bones are showing even through the jacket I made for her. And on her feet, again, are oiled rags, all soggy. Since the snows, she has been cooking at the Rouleaux's hearth, so I have not seen so much of her as before.

"Estelle, where are your boots?" I ask in French and point to her feet.

One shoulder lifts. *"Dans la rivière."*

"What do you mean, in the river?"

She shrugs again; then she mimics throwing the boots away.

"You threw them in the river, Estelle? But why?"

She only shakes her head and looks away from me. So I know. *Rouleau.*

"All of them?" I say. "Your mother's and brother's and your uncle's?"

She nods.

I think of Mr. Rouleau's high boots with their wide leather cuffs. Each has some medal pinned there.

"Take these." I slip mine off.

"Non!" She makes the throwing motion again.

"Then just wear them here. They are yours, here." I show how I can make another pair for myself. Finally, she unbinds the rags, wipes her feet with a dry cloth, and puts on the boots. They are a finger's width too large, but I shall knit her thick stockings.

"Merci, mademoiselle. *Merci!"* She smiles a smile I have never seen upon her before.

"C'est rien!" I say. *It is nothing.*

Estelle keeps glancing down at the boots as we hang clothing over poles in our new drying shed. Even with wool stockings, my feet are becoming cold from the damp earth, but I do not want her to know this. I keep hanging clothes until we are finished. Then I run through the snow to our cabin.

My thawing feet hurt. But it does not feel so bad when I think how Estelle's, now, are warm.

After supper, I tell Father and John about the boots. Father looks thunderous but says naught. John follows him in this. I know why. They do not want to give vent to anger and then have to regret their harshness against a fellow human being.

"Could we buy the slaves, Father?" John asks. "And then make them free?"

"Nay. Not here in Pennsylvania. 'Tis against our law to purchase slaves. Besides, we have naught with which to buy them."

"Then we must help them run away somewhere," I say.

Father and John regard me. The silence becomes a weight on my shoulders and heart. When I think further,

I see that by helping the slaves, we risk losing all. Even Father's freedom.

"I fear we must wait 'til spring," Father says. "The river will be open. The forest tracks . . ."

There is sorrow in his voice, and I understand. Winter can be cruel, and the slaves are ill prepared.

"Let us have our meditation," he goes on. "Answers oft arrive when least expected."

Thoughts come to do battle with peace. I see all of our savings depleted by fines. I see Father in the jail, in Wilkes-Barre. But after a long while, my thoughts get tired of driving me round and round, and so scatter. And then the quiet comes back, a good quiet. It tells me that somehow we *shall* help them.

I await further revelation, but there is only that.

Eugenie ❧

"Sylvette, *La veillée du Petit Jésus!* Last year at this time we were in France, and our King alive, and we in our château. Do you remember the garlands in the salons? The holly and fir and candles? And the bells, Sylvette? The bells ending the watch for the Child Jesus? So many bells at midnight! So joyful, despite the troubles in our country, and we knew, didn't we, that He was in our hearts." I whisper all this, for I do not wish to make Maman sad.

"How much a year can hold, Sylvette! How much sadness and loss. But this year? This coming year? Well. Let me tell you how it will be for you, *ma chérie*. You shall play in the snow tomorrow! On Christmas Day! Then you shall have a bit of Hannah's turkey. Soon there will be sun every day, Sylvette, and you shall run to the river again. And— are you listening, *chérie?* When the river is clear of ice, the Queen will arrive! Yes! And then we shall truly celebrate. There will be a *grande fête* and all manner of delicacies to eat. And the air will once again be warm, Sylvette, imagine! Warmth! Oh, and we shall dance and sit outside and tell each other wonderful stories, like this one. Only this is not a story. It is a promise!"

Hannah curtsies, bringing our evening meal, and the Yule log cake we asked her to make for us. Her eyes are red, and she seems most fatigued. Yet she smiles at me, and I at her.

Earlier, she brought our clean linens. How does she dry them, I wonder, in such weather? Snow and cloud and wind day after day and so cold, *mon Dieu,* one hardly dares go outside.

Except Hannah. And John. And Estelle. And Alain and the other two slaves. A week ago, on a blessedly windless day, we saw them dragging dead limbs out of the woods. They were up to their waists in snow. Even Comte de Sevigny, with whom Maman and I were walking, said that Rouleau has no heart. When the slaves saw us, they dropped their firewood at once to bow and curtsy. "Do you suppose," Maman asked, "they have been gathering wood all day?"

"I do not doubt it," the comte said placidly, and we walked on to our warm *maison,* where Maman invited the comte in to sit before our fire.

Truly, it does not seem right, if the infant Jesus lives in each of our hearts.

Midnight—and a bell rings out. A single bell! Maman, Papa, and I go to our window. *Mirabile dictu!* Abbé La Barre has somehow found a bell for us!

"And look, Eugenie!" Papa says. "Look!"

Papa and Maman stand aside so that I may see. A large bonfire burns in the clearing.

I turn away.

"Child, what is the matter?" Papa says.

"Oh, it is nothing. I am merely tired."

"Then you must rest."

He is hurt. He must have arranged for it. I look out the window again, for his sake.

It is a lovely sight, in its way. The flames. The falling snow. The stillness.

III

I try to excise the image of a farm cart, right at its center. But no, it refuses to be excised.

The bell rings and rings.

"If we all had boots such as Hannah's, Charlotte," Papa says, "we might go out and stand near it, and then return and leave our capacious boots for *Père Noël* to fill!"

Maman shakes her head, but she is smiling.

Standing near the bonfire is the last thing I wish, yet to have Hannah's boots! "Oh, Maman! Might I? I could take Sylvette on long walks. I'd prefer them to any number of bonbons on New Year's Day."

"Our daughter," Papa says, "will create *la nouveau mode*."

A new fashion! Sometimes Papa's lightheartedness works with Mama. I regard her.

"It will not be proper," Maman says. "Ladies will laugh at her. They will call her an Indian."

Papa says nothing. He does not wish to spoil *La veillée du Petit Jésus*. Nor do I. I turn away from the window. Papa lets our "drapery" fall back in place.

Lying in my warm alcove, I remember last year's Yule log, the centerpiece of our largest fireplace, and how sweets magically flew from it. Everything was arranged for my pleasure—always—and I, unable to imagine anything different.

Ah, Eugenie, you were so young, no?

On Christmas morning a beautiful fir tree stands in the corner of our *petite maison*, near the hearth! A garland of raisins and nuts decorates its boughs! There are pinecones as well, and also ribbons from Maman's basket.

The tree is so green.

"And see the raisins, Maman?"

"They are from the Kimbrell family," Papa says. "As are the black walnuts."

"The Kimbrells! Is there something we might give them in return?"

"I have been thinking," Papa says, "that the best gift might be to have those fines reduced or eliminated entirely."

"Oh, could you do that, *s'il te plaît?*"

"It will not be a simple matter."

"Yes, but you shall try?"

"I shall indeed. John Kimbrell has been an excellent teacher." Papa turns to Maman. "My dear, I know that my behavior has been contrary to your wishes. Forgive me. But in this America, I am learning, one needs to be strong and self-reliant. How much better if I can take care of us all, here. And then, in France, if there is no need, voilà, no need. Though I doubt that, given the changes there. You see, it is a practical matter, my dear, not philosophical. And we French have always been, under it all, a practical people. Besides, in this new world, why cling to the old restrictions and bounds? Why not find here a measure of freedom that goes hand in hand with the *new,* yes?"

Papa's words take my breath away. What about the Queen? The court? The proprieties and protocol? Perhaps Papa thinks that the Queen will not come! The thought is icy, and I shiver. Yet something within urges me to say, "And, Papa, if only we, that is, Maman and I, could take care of ourselves, somewhat, too. I mean here, in this America. And especially since we have no, that is, not many, servants." Never before, except when I was a child, has my speech been so poorly formed. "As a practical matter. Until the Queen arrives," I add for Maman's sake.

Maman closes her eyes and presses down on both eyelids with the tips of her fingers.

"Charlotte, Charlotte, our daughter is growing wiser. We might do well to listen." When Maman remains silent, Papa holds us close, one on either side of him. "What do you think of my tree?"

"Your tree, Papa?"

"*Oui!* I found it and cut it myself! Who else among us will be enjoying such a tree this morning? Ah, Charlotte, how happy it makes me to do this one small thing for you both. *Joyeux Noël!*"

"*Merci!*" I hug him with all my strength. "*Joyeux Noël,* Papa! But did you decorate it as well?"

"*Certainment!*"

Maman finally smiles, perhaps at the thought of Papa hanging her hair ribbons from the boughs.

"Now! Breakfast, and then Mass at our new chapel!"

There, too, a fresh fir tree scents the air. Papa winks at me. After Christmas Mass I sit between Maman and Papa and watch Abbé La Barre's puppets. There is the Star. There are the Three Kings following it. And little townspeople following the Three Kings to the crèche of the *Petit Jésus*.

I think of Papa alone in the woods, searching for our tree, in the snow. I think of our journey here, to America, this so-called new world. I think of the slave girl and her journey. And how she will one day go back to work on the plantation, for her despicable master. He is present in the chapel too, this morning. A Christian in name but not deed. For her, none of this is new. None of it is a beginning. For her, forever, there is just . . . the old.

Non. She shall not go back. The thought fairly astounds me, coming from I know not where! What is this slave to me? Why do I even dwell upon the matter?

I do not know! I hardly know who I am these days. If not the old Eugenie, then who? Yet something within, now, craves *more,* something more. If Papa can walk off into the woods, these American woods, with their mountain lions and wolves, and return with a tree for us, then surely I, Eugenie Annette Marie de La Roque, can do something noble as well.

Noble?

And is that not who we are, finally? *Nobles?*

When we return to our *maison,* we find a finely woven wreath of pine and fir hung upon our door. It is decorated with sprigs of bright red berries. Not holly berries—those I would recognize—but rather some berry clinging to dark thin branches.

"Did you do this, too, Papa?" I ask. "It is most beautiful!"

"*Non, chérie.* That is certainly beyond my abilities."

Maman frowns. "You see what happens in this new land of yours, Philippe?"

"It might be from Talon, *non?*"

"No one else has such a wreath."

"It is but a small gift."

"But one of great significance, perhaps."

Papa laughs. "Ah, *chérie!* You are seeing too much in it, surely."

"And you, too little," Maman retorts.

"Well, we shall be the envy of the settlement, I think."

"I can do without such envy. Remove it."

"But Charlotte, it is so fine. Even *élégant.*"

It is indeed, against the planks of our door—that green, the joyous red. I beg Maman to allow it to remain.

"Come inside!" she says. "It is too cold."

But she does not say *non.*

John Kimbrell *fils,* I think. Or Hannah. Possibly both. The thought warms me so that I do not even feel the cold.

Walking with Sylvette later, I hear a staccato jingling of bells and turn. On the avenue behind us, John Kimbrell *fils* is trotting alongside one of the big Belgian horses. It shakes its great head every so often and seems most pleased with itself. I pick Sylvette up and step nearer to the high bank of snow on one side of the avenue. My feet are wet and cold, and I am sorry for having walked so far. This evening, though, we are to play cards again with Madame de Sevigny and the Du Valliers, and so this afternoon offered the only chance for Sylvette's walk. How tired I am of piquet! I see the cards in my sleep.

So it is most pleasurable to look upon, instead, the great prancing Belgian horse. But it doesn't continue on. It stops, and John Kimbrell bows.

I can only hold Sylvette close and stare.

He gestures toward the horse. It wears, I see now, a blanket in bright colors, held on by a wide girth. There is a bough of fir tied to the horse's bridle, along with three brass bells. John goes to the side of the horse and weaves his gloved fingers together, making a step for me.

Despite all my misgivings, Sylvette and I are soon high

atop the great horse. Its back is so wide and long it seems that we rest upon a warm settee.

Majestically, we proceed up the avenue. I feel most queenly! Surely when Marie Antoinette does come, she will adore riding upon this wondrous horse, now walking so gently and smoothly.

Abbé La Barre steps out of his *maison* to wave. So does Duc d'Aversille. And so does the entire Du Vallier family. Heat rushes to my face, but I call out, *"Bon matin, bon matin!"* The Du Valliers simply gape. John Kimbrell, I realize, has unwittingly given me another gift.

He glances back at times, making certain we are still secure on our high perch. Too soon, we approach my *maison*, but John turns the horse onto a crossroad, and then another avenue, and then a different crossroad so that we have, yet, some distance to go. I consider asking him to stop so that I may walk the rest of the way. But we have been seen. And there is Florentine, coming to relay this scandal, no doubt.

Ah, Eugenie, how complicated! A mere ride upon a horse!

"Maman, Papa!" I cry as Papa helps me dismount. "My shoes became so wet, I could not resist Monsieur Kimbrell's kind offer of a ride upon this beautiful horse. Is he not wonderful?"

"Which does she mean?" Florentine says. "Man or beast?"

My heated face stings.

"Eugenie," Maman says, "come inside, please." I quickly turn back to smile at John Kimbrell before entering our *maison,* all but holding my breath. But Maman will not scold me in front of Florentine. She offers our guest tea. I change my shoes and then must sit at the table with them and suffer

Florentine's scowl when he thinks Maman and Papa will not see.

Hypocrite!

Later, the storm.

"Eugenie, you risk your future! . . . Eugenie, the Du Valliers are most concerned about your behavior! . . . Eugenie, do not act so impulsively again, I beg you!"

Eugenie . . . Eugenie . . . *Eugenie* . . . While Papa remains thoughtful.

In my heart I ask forgiveness of Maman. It was necessary, I want to say, but know that this will hurt her too much.

My punishment—a night of piquet with the censorious Du Valliers, and poor Maman valiantly trying to charm them back.

৵ Hannah

"Estelle! What is it?" I say in French and draw her into our cabin. She falls to her knees. Her head drops forward into her hands. Then she lies curled on her side, shivering.

"Estelle! Thou art ill!"

She is so slight 'tis nothing to carry her to my cot and remove the rags from her icy feet. I feel her brow. 'Tis hot. After reviving her with a cool cloth, I help her drink a cup of water before covering her. Then I must go back to my work at the hearth, turning the spit and basting the turkey in our roasting oven. Finally, I remove two apple tarts from the hearth's oven. Even from the distance of the hearth I can hear Estelle's teeth clattering against one another. But I cannot build up the fire any further without risk to my roasting turkey, so I take a heavy quilt from Father's bed and one from John's and put them atop those covering Estelle. I scoop embers into two warming pans and place them under the quilts, near her feet.

A harsh knocking, then, at the door. I go to open it, but Mr. Rouleau pushes it open himself. "Is she here?" he asks in French.

I stand dumfounded, not wanting to lie, yet wanting to.

He points to the footprints in snow. I tell him, in French, that they are mine. He pushes past me and enters our cabin. While he looks in the storeroom, I nudge the wet rags that serve as Estelle's boots under my cot. Mr. Rouleau emerges from the storeroom and looks in every corner of our cabin's common room. He glances at each of our cots. I had not drawn the curtain around mine, and my bed looks made. I hold my hand over my heart.

The pies on the table distract him from his search. He points. "Bring us these," he orders in French. I nod.

"Curtsy!" he orders.

I hesitate, but then do so.

"That's better."

The La Roques and Aversilles praise the turkey. Instead of a pie, I bring them each a custard with applesauce. Before we have our own meal, I pack baskets with custards, applesauce, bread, cheese, and slices of cooked salt pork. Then, hidden by the woods, I follow my trail around the edge of the clearing to Estelle's shelter near the river. She must have come this way. She would not have wanted to be seen by the French.

"Hoo-hoo!" I call, a few yards from Estelle and Alain's hut. *"Hoo-hoo-hoo."* The call of a great horned owl.

I leave the basket on a stump and retreat. The snow is turning a soft blue color, and pink sunset light fills the sky.

At our cabin I give Estelle bread soaked in warm tea, then Father, John, and I take our places at the table. Tonight, on this special night, Father will serve as our Elder. He says grace, and then John stands and says, "God is Love." John is seated, and I stand and repeat those words—words I have spoken each Christmas night for as long as I can remember. Tonight Mother, Suzanne, Grace, and perhaps even Richard are saying these same words at the community house, before dinner and hymns. Comforting thought—how we can still be together even while apart.

We begin our simple meal of roasted fowl with potatoes, carrots, and stewed apple, but I cannot eat much. Every limb aches, and I long only to close my eyes. I fear that I shall not be able to visit anyone tomorrow, with Father and John, not if I am ill. They won't want me within a mile. And we are supposed to have our evening meal with the Worthingtons. Well, I shall not go. And they may not want Father and John to come now, either.

After dinner and chores, Father and John go to their cots, and I lie down before the hearth. Sometime later, furious knocking wakes us all.

"Kimbrell!" Marquis Talon shouts. "Open this door!"

Father removes the thick limb from its brackets and opens the door. Two men stand there, the marquis and Mr. Rouleau, who holds a torch. "You must help Monsieur Rouleau search for a runaway slave," the marquis says in English. "She cannot have gotten far. Call several of your workers and go with monsieur."

My heart fairly lurches. With torches, they shall see the tracks leading from the salves' shelter to our cabin.

Father stands with his head bowed.

"Hurry, man!" the marquis says.

"Thou needn't search for her tonight," Father finally says in English. "She is here." He remains standing there, blocking their way.

The marquis translates these words for Mr. Rouleau, then says, "Why did you not tell Monsieur Rouleau? Do you not know that you can be severely punished for helping a slave run away?"

"She is not running away. She is ill. When she is well, she shall return to Mr. Rouleau."

Mr. Rouleau gives Father a terrible look as the marquis translates the words.

"She is pretending!" Mr. Rouleau cries in French. "She is good at that. I should know."

"Mr. Rouleau, she stayed with thee all through the troubles on thy island. I would not doubt her sincerity or good heart."

The marquis translates all of this. It does no good.

"We need her," Mr. Rouleau says. "Her place is with us."

"She shall remain here until she is well. Look to the others. See if they not be sickly, too. I understand that thou art quite stingy with thy provisions."

"Kimbrell, you go too far," the marquis says. "I will not translate that."

Father shuts the door and bars it.

"Kimbrell!" Mr. Rouleau shouts. *"Kimbrell!"*

We look at one another, but Father does not open the door again. After a time, it is quiet.

"If they come to take me, my children . . . leave. Go to the next settlement downriver. Find a way. And then return home when you can."

"And leave thou, Father?" John says.

"Aye."

1794

Janvier / January

Eugenie ᔑᔒ

We learned of the confrontation from the marquis himself—and how the Kimbrells are now guarding Estelle. So that is why Hannah abandoned us! It spoiled our New Year's Day *fête*, as we had to be satisfied with the indifferent offerings of Mary Worthington. I confess that my pique was at first quite selfish. *We* made to suffer. *Our* misfortune. Then I began to think, No, Hannah is nothing if not reliable. And she isn't necessary for guarding Estelle from Rouleau. It must be something else.

When it is time for Sylvette's morning excursion, I dress warmly and walk in the direction of the Kimbrells' cabin at the far end of the clearing. No one is anywhere about. The air is so cold that walking through it feels more like pushing through frigid water. No wind troubles the air today, and except for smoke rising from chimneys, all is still. A thick pad of snow lies atop each roof like a featherbed. Tree limbs hold white replicas of themselves. The earth, white. The river, white. The stone walls, white humps. But the sky—ah! The sky a piercing *brillant* blue. Hope steals my breath. The very colors of Versailles—and Marie Antoinette. Surely a fortuitous omen in this new year.

But not much smoke is rising from the Kimbrells' chimney. If I have learned one thing at all, in this America, it is that on such a morning smoke should be rising.

There is no answer to my knock. And the door is barred. "Hannah?" I call. "Hannah Kimbrell? Monsieur Kimbrell?"

Again, no answer.

"Hannah! It is I, Eugenie de La Roque." In French I ask her to open the door. I am suddenly ashamed. Hannah has been speaking our language, yet I have not made the slightest attempt to learn hers.

Estelle may be there, so I call out in French, "I have come by myself. I and Sylvette. What has happened? Why can you not open the door? I wish to speak with Hannah. I must know if she is well."

Inside, the bar slides off, and as the door opens slightly, a terrible stench emerges, the same as when Maman was so sick. I cover my nose and mouth.

"Hannah!" I whisper, raising my handkerchief. She is so pale, and her dark eyes appear huge. Her mouth is stained, as is her usually clean apron.

"We are ill," she says in French and motions for me to leave. Before she can bar the door again, I push it open. The *maison* is dim; the fire low. Hannah goes to her bed and lies down, but it is more like falling into it. Estelle lies near the hearth. Hannah's father and her brother are in beds along the opposite wall, both asleep—or worse.

I force myself to remain standing there, quite still. Should I go summon our abbé? But with Maman, I recall, he wasn't the least helpful.

The fire, then.

Courage, Eugenie.

I look for wood. There is none near the hearth. "Hannah? *Le bois?*"

She points to another door. I go there, open it, and find

a storeroom. Here are the logs, stacked to one side, and on the other, shelves holding food and supplies. I remove my gloves and choose, first, the kindling. This I pile atop ashes that seem warm enough. Soon threads of gray smoke rise and then the kindling bursts into flame. My stomach floats upward, but I force myself to continue building the fire, setting atop the flames larger pieces of wood. Part of me exults; part of me trembles.

I swing the iron crane outward and look into its black pot. Empty.

"*Lentilles,* mademoiselle," Hannah says from her bed.

The legumes! But where? I go back into the cold store-room and search. There is a box of dry river sand on the floor. How curious! I stoop and run fingers through this sand, discovering a number of *carottes* and several turnips, our *navets,* white and purple. Then, on a shelf, I find a crock labeled *lentils.*

So I must make soup, yes? How does one begin to make *le potage?*

With some liquid, I presume. I decide to begin with water and, yes!—there is a water bucket, half full. This I carry to the iron pot and pour some in. How heavy it is! And what a curious sensation to carry something heavy and rough to the touch! I feel a terrible strain on my fingers, hand, and arm, but there is something else, too, something I recognize as joy. I tip the crock and pour in some *lentilles.* I find a knife in the cupboard and, after wiping away the sand, slice carrots and turnips. Too late I realize that I prob-ably should be peeling the turnips, but how does one do that? An unruly turnip slips from my fingers, the knife clat-ters down, yet my fingers have escaped harm. The inexpertly cut vegetables I drop into the water, skin and all. Then I swing the crane and its pot back over the flames. I am making soup!

I take a cup of water to Hannah. She points to her father and John, and I take them water as well. When John awakens and sees me, he blanches even further, while I sense color flooding my cheeks. Then I take water to Estelle. If they are feverish, then they need water. This I also know.

"What has happened here," I ask Estelle.

In French, she tells me everything and then asks if I could find someone to feed and water the animals. John is too weak. They all are. And the cow must be milked soon. Her name is Violet.

Water. Feed. Milk.

Impossible.

"*S'il vous plaît,* mademoiselle," Estelle says. "They will sicken, otherwise."

Can you do this, Eugenie? Can you?

A covered passageway leads to a shed, and when I arrive there, the poor animals move toward me as if I were Hannah. At our château I watched our servants feeding chickens when I was a child. And I saw them feed hay to our milk cows, too. So what do all apprentices do when they are learning from a master? They imitate, of course!

And thus the chickens and the rooster are fed the cracked grain I find in a bin. The cow, the sheep, and the goats get dried grasses. All of them get water. But the cow—she does not want her food. She wants to be milked.

I must find Rachel Stalk or Mary. I look down at my ruined shoes. I think of the snow. The cow gives a loud bellow, and I back away from her. She turns to reproach me.

Ah, *mon Dieu,* how difficult can it be?

I take a bucket hanging from a peg, but it seems that it is not I doing this; rather, someone else. Then this someone else, who is somehow still me, is stooping, her face right up against the cow's heaving side with its rough fur. This person gently grips a swollen teat and moves her hand downward as I seen a little dairymaid once do, to my intense embarrassment, then. Tears come. The cow moans although not as loudly as before. "Do not cry, Madame Violette. See? I am trying my best. I, Eugenie Annette Marie de La Roque, your milkmaid. Do not cry *s'il vous plaît,* but allow me to have all your milk now."

Strangely, my voice seems to calm her, and the milk flows. Streams of it steaming into the bucket!

"*Merci,* madame," I sing to her.

Someone touches my shoulder and I turn my head a little, fear coursing through me.

It is John Kimbrell fils, saying something I cannot understand. Then he gestures for me to leave. Hardly able to keep himself upright, he clutches a post.

I shake my head. I have found the necessary rhythm, and the poor cow's milk is flowing well. My face has never held more heat—*to be seen like this.* But there is something else, too, something I recognize as pride.

When the milk finally stops flowing into the bucket, the cow seems to give a great sigh. Her flank heaves outward against my cheek and then inward again. "I think she will be well now," I say in French as I stand and rearrange my gown. "You must rest. Go, go!" I point to the door.

Still clutching the post, he leans forward to take the bucket of milk. Then he brushes at the air between us as if hoping to cleanse it. "Go!" I command, and he totters into the storeroom with the milk.

I raise my hand to my shoulder and hold it there a moment, but remove it when John reenters the shed with a different bucket and a cloth. He points to the cow, then seats himself on a small stool and begins washing her. It is too much for him, this up-and-down motion, and he tips forward, against her side.

"Monsieur Kimbrell!" I help him up and after a while we walk, slowly, back into the *maison*.

Estelle motions me over to her. Could I not find some way to help her people? She fears for them, now. "*L'abbé*, mademoiselle, *s'il vous plaît!*"

I nod.

"Bless you, my lady. You are so good!"

I fill a cup of water for each of them and leave it nearby. I take Hannah's slate and draw a picture of the deerskin boots and point to my feet. When she understands what I am asking, she nods. I also take the crock of lentils from the shelf in the pantry and two carrots from the bin of sand and hold these up before her. Again, she nods. I bring three logs from the storeroom, one at a time, and place them by the hearth.

Before leaving, I stir the soup as I have seen our Louisa do. Then I remember.

Chamber pots.

Impossible!

I stand there until, somehow, I am moving. Carrying water outside, in the bucket. Carrying the chamber pots to the far end of the yard. There must be some other, proper place for the waste, but I know not where. One by one I empty the pots and then pour a little water into them.

It is the most awful thing I have done in my life.

Then, in Hannah's boots, I fly to Abbé La Barre's cabin, Sylvette barking and running alongside.

Bless you, my lady. You are so good.

At Versailles we flattered one another as a matter of custom. Ah, you are so beautiful! Ah, how clever! How delightful! What a superb gown! Ah, how good you are! We expected such words, even implicitly demanded them; to receive, you must give. And though these hyperboles were false most of the time, or at least bereft of the full truth—and we all aware of that—we still delighted in hearing them. But now I can see how different Estelle's words are—rich and deep with conviction and truth, like a Chinese gong struck once, with force. At the court, our flatteries must have floated through the air like the glissando of a glass harmonica.

Struggling to breathe and talk at the same time, I tell Abbé La Barre about the Kimbrells and Estelle and the other slaves. He throws on his cloak. He will, he says, inform the marquis himself.

Outside, the cold no longer seems cold. The day is still all blue and white. At our *maison,* I heat water and clean my hands. Then I scrutinize them. They do not look bad. In fact, they still look like my own hands. Pink and white and finely formed, the fingernails clean and pretty.

I am still myself.

Only, some new person, too.

Maman weeps at the sight of me, in Hannah's boots, in a soiled gown, my hair disordered. That I am making a pot of soup for us only increases her misery. Papa tries to console her, but it is futile.

"We thought wild animals had eaten you, Eugenie!"

"But Maman, I had to help them. Who else will?"

"Why could you not have told Talon, instead of going there yourself?"

Because . . . because I was right there and it was . . . urgent. But I say nothing, for she would not like those words.

"He is responsible for them, Eugenie. Not you. Why must you dishonor us? Running back and forth across the settlement! Soiling your clothing! Endangering yourself! Your gown we cannot save. Your redingote we must, and your shoes. But how shall we clean them? Whoever saw you must think you have gone mad. The Du Valliers—"

"Charlotte, Charlotte," Papa murmurs. "I shall clean them."

"And what if we ourselves become ill? Daughter, you were not thinking—again!"

"Maman," I finally say. "I helped because she helped us."

"It was her responsibility to do so."

"And so, too, ours?"

"Oh, my child."

"Maman, please have some of the soup, anyway. Then maybe you shall feel better."

"She is right, Charlotte. The mind is not happy, sitting atop an empty stomach."

"It will only make me feel worse."

This night I think upon all that I have done today. I have milked a cow. I have built a fire. I have made soup. I have cared for the sick. I have done more in this one day, it seems, than in all my previous life. And now, as I listen to the wind—so much like waves beating against these logs—I am happy. I am truly happy! It has been months, many months, since I have felt happy. It is almost a new sensation entirely. I wish I could tell Maman. Perhaps I can tell Papa. Holding Sylvette's paws, I lean back into the warmth of it.

But then, Abbé La Barre comes with the news that two of Monsieur Rouleau's slaves have died four days ago— Estelle's mother and the elderly man named Jacques, who was Estelle's uncle. Her brother is still alive, though quite weak. He tells us, too, that there is talk of imprisoning the Kimbrells. All of them.

Mon Dieu! Papa is frowning. Maman says, "And well they should be imprisoned! They are far too disruptive."

"But Maman . . ."

"Hush, child."

After Abbé La Barre leaves, Maman says, "Now we shall all die."

ᴄᴄ Hannah

Again comes the pounding against our door. It can only be Mr. Rouleau.

'Tis—with Marquis Talon. As they enter our cabin, Marquis Talon says, "we need her, Kimbrell. It's time she returns."

Father speaks in a calm voice. "She is not yet strong enough. Take her now and she may only become ill again."

The marquis translates all that into French, and then Mr. Rouleau's reply into English. "I need more help than just the one slave!" Mr. Rouleau shouts.

"Mr. Rouleau. You have two daughters who might help you, if they be well. Also, there be others here at the settlement to hire."

Mr. Rouleau stamps his foot. "The one slave shall do it all, then, and if anything happens to him, the fault lies at your feet, sir! As for me, I shall make a full report to the vicomte."

"Indeed thou must," Father says. "It would be wise to let him know how a lack of care has caused the deaths of the man named Jacques and of Estelle and Alain's mother. The vicomte can then advise others who come here seeking sanctuary. The bodies must be properly buried. I am sure Abbé La Barre has told you this as well."

"And I will tell you the same thing I told him. In this cold? With the earth like iron? We have already carried the bodies into the forest and left them. Good day, sir. You shall hear more of this matter quite soon."

Father steps outside, blocking the man's way. "The remains must be properly buried. We shall dig below the frost, my son and I. Tell us where thou hast taken the bodies."

Mr. Rouleau's eyes shift away. "No doubt it is already too late."

"Thou art a dishonorable man."

"And you are a thief who shall be made to pay for your thievery." Mr. Rouleau steps around Father.

"Kimbrell," the marquis says, "you are meddling! The girl is properly Rouleau's. You must stop interfering with the affairs of the French."

"I shall give her up only when she is well."

"Then I'll have no choice but to punish you. Do you understand me?"

"I do."

"Very well then."

"John," Father says after he bars the door. "There has been no new snow. It should be easy enough to find the tracks."

"Do not despair," Father says to Estelle. "Thy mother and thy uncle shall be buried and the graves properly marked. And there shall be prayers." Explanatory gestures accompany the words.

Estelle merely nods her head. John begins to dress in his warmest clothing.

"Father," I say. "If John goes, then Mr. Rouleau may see him and call someone to stop him." I cannot bring myself to say the word *imprison*. "Why not let me go? I must still cook for the French, so they won't harm me."

Father considers this. "I cannot allow it. Yet it may be best for me to remain here. But then—"

"I won't go too near, Father. Just to mark the place before I get Mr. Stalk."

"John, go with her," he finally says. "Stand guard there. Hannah will get Mr. Stalk to relieve thee. When he does, come back here, both of you. We will find a way to bury them. Go through the woods rather than across the settlement."

I lift the rifle down from its pegs and fill the powder chamber. Then I take flint box, cartridges, and rifle, and we walk out into the cold.

My trail to Estelle's shelter serves us well. The snow has been trampled by foraging deer and we can walk quickly. When we near the shelter, we turn eastward, thinking we might see other tracks.

Aye. Here they are. Lines upon the snow tell us that the bodies were dragged. Who did this? One of the workers? If so, he has not much honor.

We walk for several more minutes and then come upon wolf prints going in the same direction. John takes the rifle, and we walk on. Wind high up in the great pines and hemlocks makes a heavy thrumming. I am saddened to think of Estelle's mother and uncle having to come so far from their home only to die here. And I am afraid now of what we will find.

The trail ends some hundred paces into the woods, where we soon come upon what I do not want to see. The disturbed white mounds. The strewn-about blankets and red-flecked snow.

"Hannah," John whispers. "Do not look upon this."

I turn away and utter a prayer.

Father had not been thinking—I blame the illness. He would not have wanted us to see this. But I forgive him. And the wolves and mountain lions and bobcats. They do only what instinct tells them to do. Unlike our own kind. Rouleau, I cannot forgive.

Trees creak and groan in the wind. I will not hear the wolves or the mountain lions should they return. But no fear enters me. There is no room, sadness and outrage filling the whole space.

My expression must give it away. Estelle cries out when I return.

I hold Estelle while she sobs. "Father, she cannot go back to him."

"Aye." But there is a measure of hopelessness in his voice.

Estelle moves away from me and wraps her shawl close about her. "I must be with Alain," she says in French.

I go to stop her, but Father says 'tis best for her to be with her brother now.

Carrying a basket with bread, preserves, dried fish, and applesauce, Estelle slowly makes her way to the trail skirting the clearing.

"She will go there, Father. 'Tis near sunset, and the wolves—"

"I think not. She will stay with Alain."

"Then they will both go. I cannot bear to think of it!"

"Hannah, calm thyself. I will follow to make certain they do not. John, stay here with Hannah. But first, I am sorry. I should not have let thee go. Forgive me, my daughter."

"I already have, Father. But I cannot forgive Rouleau."

"Thou must. Otherwise, what good our beliefs? Ah, my Hannah. 'Tis a high wall to scale. All of it."

'Tis nigh midnight. Father has not returned. John and I regard the fire. To speak will only give voice to fear, so we are silent. My hands shake so. Wolves bark and yip, chasing something. Then that unfortunate creature shrieks wildly. I cover my ears. When I uncover them, it is quiet.

"Hannah," John says, "fear not. He is with Mr. Stalk."

I say naught but know what must have happened.

Eugenie ⁊

"Enough! The marquis did what was required. The Americans are here to serve us, not to conduct our affairs."

"But Maman, did not Monsieur Kimbrell wish merely to help the ill girl and properly bury the others?"

"It was not his place to do so. He must be taught a lesson . . . and serve as an example for the other Americans."

"Papa! What do you think?"

"I think that Talon will lose his best worker if he keeps him locked up. What is the point of it?"

"The point, Philippe," Maman says, "is propriety."

"Will it not stir up the Americans against us?" I ask.

"We shall see," Papa says.

Then Hannah enters with our dinner, and a wondrous scent fills our *maison* as she serves a *ragoût* and warm bread after curtsying to each of us. Her eyes are tinged red. Her face, blotched and swollen. "Hannah," I say, to Maman's acute displeasure. "How is your father?" These words are in French, but she understands.

"Not well," she replies in our language. "John, though, is with him now."

John. "But why?"

"The marquis ordered it."

"Then you are all alone?"

"Eugenie," Maman warns.

When she leaves, Maman scolds me for speaking with

Hannah. Papa comes to my defense and then says, "This affair, Charlotte, reflects badly upon us. I will not be surprised if all the Americans leave, come spring."

"Let them."

"Charlotte, Charlotte. They are not our peasants. Do not blame them, I beg you, for what they did not do."

"Like the slaves, Papa. They do not deserve blame for anything, either."

Maman stares at me a moment before turning to Papa. "Look what this America is doing to your daughter, Philippe!"

"I see."

"You must speak to her."

Later, after Maman falls asleep, he does.

"*Ma chérie,* your father is proud of you."

"Papa! Truly?"

"Truly. You have traveled far."

It takes me awhile to understand that he does not mean in actual distance.

"What about Hannah?" I whisper. "And Monsieur Kimbrell? And . . . John? Is there anything we can do, Papa?"

"I have approached Talon about the matter but to no avail. He sees it as a test of wills."

"And Maman. She is so unhappy with me. Papa? I greatly dislike Florentine even though he is one of us. He is reveling in all this."

"Hush, *ma petite.*"

"But it is true!"

He kisses me on the brow and bids me sleep.

The wind is fierce tonight, my poor word *fierce* hardly expressive of its fury. It seems almost sentient as it gathers itself, becoming greater, ever greater, and then crashes against our *maison* with the force of an avalanche. And it has been snowing so hard! I gather Sylvette close but cannot sleep for thinking of the Kimbrells in their prison and the two slaves in their rude hut.

Morning tames the vicious wind, and Hannah arrives with our breakfast and something else—boots for all of us. It is finally Papa who invites her to speak.

"Who has made these fine boots, Hannah?"

She answers in French. "My father and my brother, comte."

"They are well made!" He rubs the suede leather, the fringe at the top.

"They are for you, comte, and for madame and mademoiselle."

"I do not wish to wear boots," Maman says in our language, except for the word *boots,* which she gives an angry emphasis. "They are for savages."

"May I wear mine, Maman? Just to take Sylvette outside? It is impossible otherwise, with all this snow."

"Permit it, Charlotte. We all have had too much of our *petite maison.*"

Maman finally permits. More than that, she even smiles, but it is because she is lapsing into memory gain. "Do you know," she says, "Marie Antoinette loved the snow when she was a child in Austria? Perhaps she will like it here after all."

"Kimbrell can make her a pair of boots, too," Papa says, "and you can go off on some mountaineering adventure."

Maman's smile fades. "If she comes."

"She shall!" I quickly say. "Won't she, Papa?" I slip on

my boots, delighted by their softness and the fact that my gown nearly hides them from view so Maman won't be too offended.

"She shall indeed come," Papa says. But I hear something in his voice and quickly regard him. The tone is too emphatic, as if he were speaking to children who need reassurance.

"Come, Sylvette." I take my cloak. Hannah has left, and we haven't even thanked her.

Outside, I see her on the avenue. At first I take small quick steps. Soon I am running—forgetting everything for a moment but the sudden pleasure of it.

"Hannah!" I say, coming alongside her. I have to catch my breath. *"Merci!"*

She smiles a little.

"But why," I ask, "when we are so . . . uncivil to you?" Does she understand my French? She simply keeps walking toward the *maison* being used as a small prison. I stop and let her go. She must be taking them food.

But no. She merely touches the door with one hand, and waits awhile. Does she try to speak with them? Soon she is walking away, with her pots.

The small prison's window is barred shut on the outside, like its door. A thin line of smoke rises from the chimney. I approach the *maison* and go right up to the door itself. Sylvette barks, announcing our presence. *"Messieurs,"* I say loudly. *"C'est Eugenie de La Roque. Merci! Merci beaucoup!"*

There is no response.

Trembling, I step away.

We walk to the river, Sylvette and I. It looks like a field of snow. In the boots, my feet are warm.

1794

Février / February

Hannah

Here's love by the handful, here's love by the ball. Here's love for the Elders. Here's love for you all.

Lines from the song come to me almost in mockery. I feel no love except for Father, John, and our family. I do not want to stay here! They won't even let me take Father and John their meals. I fear I am beginning to hate the nobles. They are not noble, but small and stingy and cruel.

This love it flows freely from this little store. To all Mother's children the wilderness o'er.

Flames on the hearth burn hard and angry, drawn upward by the wind.

I cannot sleep, and then when I do, I cannot awaken, each dawn.

The girls here avoid me, even while we hang linen on the lines strung between sycamores near the river when the drying shed is full. They chatter with one another and pretend I am not there. Have the nobles told them not to speak with me? Are they afraid? Today is sun-filled and mild, with no wind, a day to cheer the heart—only mine cannot be cheered. Estelle approaches with a bucket and fills it from a hole in the river ice. Passing quite close to me with her full bucket, she whispers that she is to leave soon.

"When?" I whisper back. Mary and Rachel are watching us.

She looks out over the ice-and-snow-covered river. "Soon." Tears hang like little icicles at her eyelashes.

"Back to the plantation?"

"*Non.* New Orleans. We will be sold at the slave market there."

"Sold? This cannot be!"

Her eyes round and she stiffens. I turn. 'Tis Mademoiselle de La Roque, approaching. She walks well, and she looks younger without the white powder on her face.

"*Bonjour!*" mademoiselle calls.

The other girls all curtsy. Estelle and I also curtsy, causing the girls to giggle foolishly. My heart feels stony.

"*Le Printemps*, Hannah! *Le Printemps est arrive!*" Spring is here!

I look across the river where tree limbs have taken on a red hue. "*Non,*" I say. "*Février.*"

'Tis just like her not to care that I shall be the one fined if Madame de La Roque hears of this exchange. Nor does she notice Estelle's unhappiness. She is too busy teasing Sylvette with a branch. Estelle curtsies and begins walking back with her full bucket of water.

Mademoiselle de La Roque looks up. "*Au revoir!*" she calls. Estelle turns and curtsies. She raises a hand to her eyes before hurrying away.

"What is the matter with her?" Mademoiselle de La Roque asks in French.

"She leaves soon," I reply slowly in French. "She and her brother will be sold in a place called New Orleans."

"Oh, Hannah!"

"They leave when the river is clear of ice."

She comes close, despite our audience, and says, "Perhaps we can find some way to help."

We help them escape? My heartbeat quickens. *Nous,* in French. Does she mean her family will help? Or the nobles? Or—the two of us? But all this I do not know how to say in French.

"We create a plan," she goes on. "Every escape first begins with a plan."

"The two of us?"

"*Oui!*"

The thought fairly sets me shaking. Only at the last minute do I remember to curtsy as she turns to leave.

"Hannah," she begins, but then does not say anything further.

The stoniness inside has become fear. Who can trust any noble? I think of Father and John in that little prison and tears come again. I cannot put them in more danger, can I? And yet, would not Father want Estelle and Alain to escape from Rouleau?

A word comes to me. *Sanctuary.*

My knees quake yet I am able to run back to our cabin. There I set about making a large apple tart. When it is ready, I carry it to the marquis's *maison* and rap on the door with the stone knocker.

He opens it himself—the marquis!—in a blue velvet frock coat very like General Washington's. A fire burns well on the hearth. Books are upon his table, and inkpot and quill. He has been writing, and I disturb him. Words refuse to form.

"What is this?" he asks, as if I hold some strange creature. "Enter."

'Tis a very command. I close the door and place the tart upon his table but well away from the books. I nearly forget to curtsy.

"Ah! You are learning your lesson, Hannah Kimbrell. Now tell me. Do you wish to plead for your father and your brother, with this tart?"

I should!

"I forewarn you. It will do no good. They must remain where they are until they learn *their* lesson. And what is their lesson, Hannah?"

"I know not, Marquis Talon."

"Of course you do. Think."

My knees are quaking again, and my jaw. "'Tis not to . . . meddle in thy affairs."

"Indeed. But now I suspect that you are here to do just that."

Before leaving, I remember to curtsy.

"Wait," he commands. "I wish to know why you hoped to bribe me with this." He points to the tart, now scenting the room with cinnamon. "Tell me."

The marquis is smiling!

"Your . . . Excellency, I came to ask thee to . . . grant the slaves . . . sanctuary here and . . . your protection."

"Aha! More meddling. I knew it, did I not? And you believe that I am able to protect them?"

I can only nod. Tears have welled up.

"You flatter me, child. That, I cannot do. They are not mine. They are the property of Monsieur Rouleau, and he will be leaving with them as soon as there is transport."

"But thou," I hear myself saying, "represent . . . the Queen of France."

"Ho! A discussion, now, on what? The law? Monarchic privilege?" The marquis goes to his table and sits. "Since you have been forbidden to see your father and your brother, I can only assume you have come to this thought yourself. True?"

I nod again.

"Stop bobbing your head. You have a voice. Answer my question."

"I . . . I have come to it myself."

"Then I admire your intellectual effort but must repeat that I can do nothing in this regard. You have baked this wonderful tart for naught."

Nothing is ever for naught, my dear Hannah. We simply do not have eyes to see, yet.

"Pour me some coffee and cut a piece of this."

I look about the cabin, which is twice as large as our own. The marquis possesses a sideboard where plates are stacked and cutlery fills a drawer. I do as he bids and then go to the door again.

He eats.

"Do you miss them? Your father and your brother?"

I cannot trust my voice. I nod again.

"Stop that. Do you miss them?"

"I do, Excellency."

"Are you faring all right on your own?"

"I . . . am."

"*Bon.* This is delicious, by the way. You are to be congratulated. Now, go. I have work to do."

Outside, the mild air soothes my face, but the ache of failure feels like something wanting to crush my very bones.

1794

Mars / March

Eugenie ❧

"Sylvette! *Non!*"

But she bounds, barking, toward the river, where cakes of ice are sliding rapidly by on brown water. Does she think they are hares afloat on the river?

"Sylvette!"

One piece floats toward the landing, and before I can reach the river's edge, Sylvette has leaped atop it, barking furiously.

"Sylvette, jump into the water. Come back!!"

She will not. I know she will not. She likes to play with the water but does not swim in it. *Mon Dieu*. Already the river is taking her swiftly away. Her barking is becoming fainter.

She turns toward me, and I fear that she will jump. But the river is too fast, too strong. She shall drown!

"Wait, Sylvette. Wait!"

A large piece of ice skims close to the landing. I step onto it and then slide away, too.

The settlement falls behind us. There are just woods to either side. As fast as I go, Sylvette goes even faster on her smaller piece of ice.

Our Lady, help us.

Water ripples over the edges of the ice cake. When I shift my weight, the ice tilts. I must stand exactly in the center.

Eugenie, think, now!

That settlement. The one we passed in the autumn. Surely, someone will see. I will have to call out loudly as we pass.

There's a larger piece of ice just ahead and I leap to it. But all the rest are small. My gown is sopping at the bottom, and heavy.

Be patient, Eugenie. Use your head. Do not think of the water below you. What matters is Sylvette.

She is still barking.

At a bend in the river, Sylvette's piece of ice slides against others and slows. Oh, if only I had one of those poles Papa used last autumn. Then I see, floating quite near, a branch. Though it is not a pole, it may suffice.

I crouch down, wetting more of my gown, and grab for the limb. The water is so cold that it scalds, but I have the branch. I have it!

Bon! Now what?

I try to push with it, but the river is too deep. Still, I hang on to it as my meager raft bobs and bounces downriver. My hands, in their wet gloves, are becoming numb. Soon I will not be able to grip the branch at all.

Our Lady, I must save Sylvette! Help me do this, please.

The brown water froths onward, but ahead, at another bend, the river appears all white. As I approach, I see jumbled ice heaped there. My piece rushes toward the pile, but where is Sylvette? Crouched, I await the *débâcle*. It comes with a jarring crash that spills water all over my boots, gown, and redingote.

"Sylvette! Sylvette!"

At her loud barking, I turn.

Ah! She is at the edge of the ice pile and quite near shore. Seeing the branch, she races over the pile toward me and soon has the end of it in her jaw, as if all this were simply a variation of our old game. The pile suddenly groans, falling into individual chunks again. But Sylvette has the branch, and her piece of ice is approaching mine. "Sylvette, *ma petite,* come!" I get the branch from her, and she leaps to my side. Then I plunge the branch down into the brown water, and it touches bottom. *Do as Papa did, Eugenie. Push! Push!*

Great chunks and heaps of ice resume their swift journey. Ours desires to go with them. I push harder. Now only a few feet of brown water separate us from a snowy rise. I let the branch go and, holding Sylvette, jump.

We nearly slip back into the river but finally lie there, in the snow, both of us shaking. Are we on the right side of the river? I am not certain. And how far from that settlement? Again, I do not know. The snow is both wet and deep, and my feet are as numb as my hands.

Without losing hold of Sylvette, I get up and make my way through a stand of large trees where the snow is not so deep and then come out onto the bank of the river again. I must not allow it out of my sight. Tree limbs slide by, and pieces of ice. Otherwise, it is so quiet.

I must get warm—but how? With stiffened fingers, I tear off my gloves and blow on my hands. I stamp my feet. I make so much noise, I nearly do not hear the faint calling. I look downriver—no. I look upriver, and yes, something— the skiff!—approaches.

"Mademoiselle!"

"Here!" I cry out in French. "Sylvette! Bark, please!"

She does, and as the skiff quickly approaches, I shout as loudly as I can and wave. Never before have I done such shouting. The skiff angles toward shore and nearly slides past, but Hannah—yes, it is Hannah!—directs it toward the bank and throws me a rope. I cannot feel it in my hands but somehow wind it around a near tree and let the tree moor the boat. Holding something, Hannah jumps out and climbs the small bank. The mooring rope goes taut as the boat spins to the side, wanting to fly with the river.

Hannah speaks not a word but wildly tears at branches she finds lying on the snow, snapping and cracking them. She strips dry leaves off them. Her hands are shaking, but somehow she creates a fire by laying ashes from a pan upon the leaves.

She tells me by gesture and her oddly pronounced French how she happened to hear Sylvette's barking and saw her jump onto the piece of ice. Then she saw me follow on another ice cake. She pantomimes hanging linen. Then she points to the pan and says, "Estelle."

Again I understand. Rouleau's *maison* is near the river. If Estelle and Hannah were nearby, hanging linen, Hannah might have observed it all and told Estelle to run for the pan of embers while she herself got the skiff. She anticipated, like a master at chess. She gambled like the shrewdest gamblers in the gaming rooms that there would be time enough to get the pan and skiff and find us.

"*Merci*, Hannah," I say, tears blurring the scene before me.

The fire's heat soon thaws my fingers and toes and it is time to go. But we cannot use the skiff—the river's current is too strong. We will leave the skiff tied there and walk back, Hannah explains—to my relief. I am not eager to go upon the river again, in any kind of conveyance.

Hannah leads, breaking us a trail. Some time later, we hear voices calling and return the shouts. Then Papa appears with several others, including the marquis, and rushes ahead to embrace me before bowing to Hannah and declaring her a heroine of the greatest magnitude.

"Mademoiselle is the brave one," Hannah tells Papa. He shakes his head. *Foolish!* I know he wants to say, but will not insult Hannah now. "Name your reward, Hannah Kimbrell, and I will do my best to grant it."

I look to Hannah, whose eyes are now filling.

"No," she begins. "'Tis enough . . ." She continues in French, "The deed enough."

"If it were not for those boots, Charlotte!" Papa keeps saying. Exulting, really.

"If it were not for the boots, Philippe, she would not have jumped upon that piece of ice in order to chase that disobedient dog."

"But Charlotte, she is safe. Hannah Kimbrell saved our daughter."

Never before have I seen Papa so joyful. All evening people have been coming to the marquis's *maison* to hear the story. Maman dressed my hair and took out Grand-mère's necklace for me to wear with my favorite blue gown. It is almost as if we are in attendance upon the Queen.

Comte and Comtesse d'Aversille smile with Papa and commend "their" Hannah Kimbrell. The Sevignys and Du Valliers say little, however. I am hopeful that this latest feat of mine will finally, and forever, dampen Florentine's ardor and dissuade his parents from any further thoughts of a match.

But Florentine comes close, his scornful smile in place. "So, mademoiselle," he says in a low voice, "were you pretending to be an American Indian out there?"

"I was indeed. How did you ever guess?"

"You are, apparently, quite talented."

"Do you think so, Florentine? You see, I am working on some amusing entertainment for our Queen."

"I'm certain she shall be quite amused."

"Oh, I'm pleased to hear that you think so. Your opinion means so much to me."

"Indeed? Then you might be further pleased to know that I have not forgotten about your peasant, Kimbrell fils."

"Ah, yes. And the Queen, I'm sure, shall be most delighted to know of his sister Hannah's *courage.* And now excuse me, please. I must speak with Hannah."

"Of course. You must not keep your heroine waiting."

"Thank you, Florentine. You are most understanding."

Clash, clank go our swords. But I am determined not to allow him to ruin this evening for me.

Passing near Hannah, who is serving apple cider, I say, in English, "Hannah, I am . . . happy tonight." The marquis taught me the words, and I am most proud of myself for having learned them.

"I am also happy, mademoiselle," she says in English. She may well be though she hardly looks it.

Then I must revert to French. "You and Estelle saved us. So now, truly, it is my turn."

Her eyes darken. She nods slightly. "*Oui,* mademoiselle."

"Eugenie."

"*Oui,* Mademoiselle Eugenie." She curtsies.

"So she can curtsy!" Florentine says, suddenly at my side again.

"And in the most novel ways, with her deeds, in fact."

She curtsies with her deeds. The thought—no, the revelation—has just come. I see her rushing toward me with the pan of embers. I see her breaking branches and gathering leaves and with trembling fingers creating a fire, there on the snow.

"Well, she does not curtsy to me," Florentine says, "either in form or in deed. You, mademoiselle, obviously possess superior charms."

I look at Florentine in disbelief, for I hear tenderness in his words, and not scorn. But then he adds, in his more customary tone, "Perhaps you might use those charms to better instruct your—what shall I call her?—*servant*, still?"

"Ah, Florentine. You do not change, do you."

"And why should I, mademoiselle?"

"Of course you should not, perfect as you are."

"You flatter me."

"That is my end in life, Florentine."

"A truly noble one."

"Indeed!"

"Attention! Attention!" the marquis calls. "I must make an announcement."

The marquis waits until all is quiet. He is standing alongside the hearth, his face pink from the heat of the fire in the overly warm room.

"But first . . . Comte de La Roque, open the door, please!"

Papa does so and there stand John Kimbrell père and fils. A gasp arises from all of us. Hannah moves toward them as best she can in this crowded room. When they embrace, we applaud.

"At Comte de La Roque's request," the marquis says, "I have pardoned the Kimbrells for meddling in the affairs of Monsieur Rouleau. So be it. They are now free to . . . work!"

We laugh and applaud again. The marquis notices, I am certain, that the Kimbrells do not bow to us, yet he says nothing. At least not tonight. Fear for them burns away the happiness. John Kimbrell surveys the room until he sees me. In the next moment, he is looking at Hannah again.

The Du Valliers begin murmuring. Florentine says, "I believe a duel is most certainly necessary."

"Talon will never permit it."

"And he will know?"

"I will tell him."

"So I am right. He is your *Américain* courtier."

"Florentine, you struggle too hard to spoil my evening. Just your being here is sufficient."

The *coup d'état*. He moves roughly away, and I know for certain that I have made an enemy. Hannah turns to curtsy and then all three Kimbrells leave. I lower my face to Sylvette, who has been deemed naughty by everyone in the room. She whines, wanting down, but I refuse to indulge her.

Then Papa is there, alongside me. "*Merci*, Papa," I whisper. "*Merci.*"

✑ *Hannah*

John and I work in silence as we settle the animals for the night. When our chores are finished, he sits on the narrow bench where we change our boots before entering the cabin. But he doesn't bend forward to unlace his boots. I sit alongside him. Can he sense my thoughts? Does he know what I have been longing to tell him these past days?

"Hannah," he says, "Gabriel Stalk told us a flotilla may arrive tomorrow. Word has come from downriver."

"Tomorrow!"

"Aye."

"The *Queen?*"

"The messenger said naught about any queen aboard."

"Will those boats then take the Rouleau family and their slaves?"

"Not right away, but after the flotilla returns from upriver."

"John, if 'tis the Queen, how shall we . . . be? Must I curtsy and you bow? I do not wish to hurt Father any further."

"We will be who we are, Hannah."

"And if 'tis the Queen, John, Eugenie will just go back to being like she was."

"Then she will be who she is, too. Only more so. I'm such a fool. To have any sort of hope, I mean."

"Oh, John, I, too, have had . . . hope." I worry my fingers some. The need to tell my brother everything finally overwhelms prudence.

"John, she says she wishes to help the slaves. At least she tells me so. Can it be?"

He turns to regard me, his face all surprise. I tell him how, after the rescue, she wanted to reward Estelle, too. How she asked my help. How we haven't formed a plan yet. How I haven't told Father anything. All these words, wanting out of the cage, fly wildly. "But John, I don't know if I can . . . trust her."

"Why not?"

"Because . . . she is a noble."

He is quiet for a long while. Finally he says, "I believe thou can, Hannah."

"Thou wishes to believe it."

"Aye. I do. And I will help thee."

"Oh, John. I wanted thee clear of it." My fingers are back to being little chicks pecking at grain.

"Well, I'm not, now."

"John, she will always be an . . . aristocrat."

"Aye."

My brother puts his arm around my shoulder and holds on. 'Tis good not to be alone in it anymore. I will not think of the danger. I will just give thanks for this moment.

Eugenie ❧

Comte de Sevigny shouts out something as he and the comtesse hurry past our *maison*. Then the Du Valliers rush by. "The Queen!" Du Vallier calls. "The Queen!"

We throw on our cloaks. I slip into my boots and pick up Sylvette. Maman and I hurry out into warmth and sunlight. Even the elderly Comte and Comtesse d'Aversille are hurrying, aided by their walking sticks. We make our own stream flowing to the Susquehanna.

"Sylvette! At last!" Joy blends with fear. What will she think of this place? And of us, now? I want to run but must wait for Maman. Our steps are so slow it is maddening. Then here is Papa. And all the workers. For a moment it seems we are at the racetrack near Paris, everyone crushing together, eyes widely open, breath held.

A shout goes up as three longboats come clearly into view. "Oh, Maman! Marie Antoinette!" Sylvette wriggles down, but I pick her up again so that she might be among the first to see our Queen.

"Eugenie! Sylvette is soiling your cloak! Set her down."

I see no dirt against the dark of the cloak but obey Maman. There is so much fear in her voice, it charges through me as well. Our hair neither powdered nor dressed, clogs (and my boots!) clumped with earth, few jewels to be seen, the hems of our gowns stained brown where they drag in the mud each day. Imagining this moment, I have never envisioned it to be quite like this.

Then Hannah and John arrive. *Courage,* Hannah's smile seems to say. John glances in our direction but turns away quickly. I raise my handkerchief to Hannah after dabbing my eyes. Despite my fear, despite our poor appearance, despite everything, this still feels like a beginning, new and wonderful. And how much more so than when we arrived last November.

But where . . .

"Are there no banners?" I ask. "No flag?"

"Perhaps, because this is America," Maman whispers.

The boats appear to be the same as those in which we traveled upriver—simple longboats riding low in the water. Two with canopies, and one open. But three? Only three for the Queen and her entourage?

High above the river, wild geese form an arrowlike shape wavering northward. A good omen, I tell myself.

"Form two lines," the marquis calls. "Workers, move back. Farther, farther!"

Hannah and John and the other workers walk back up the landing and stand in a group to one side while we form two well-spaced lines. In my thoughts I practice my curtsy, but then cold rushes through me. Hannah. Hannah and John and Monsieur Kimbrell. I whisper my concern to Papa that the Kimbrells will not demonstrate proper etiquette, and Papa goes to the marquis. After a moment, the marquis breaks from our line and strides over to the workers. The Kimbrells leave. Then as the boats turn toward the landing, the marquis walks forth to be the first to greet our Queen.

Nobles step from the boats, as clumsy as we were. This

cannot be proper. Surely the Queen must be the first to set foot upon this land. Is she within a closed compartment? Could she be ill from the voyage? I wonder, too, if it will be easier to approach her, here. She has always been surrounded by so many attendants—the ladies of honor, the chambermaids and pages and butlers, the ministers and secretaries and doctors, and she the center of it all. So encircled! I remind myself not to address her until she first speaks to me.

Six courtiers and six ladies disembark from the first boat, their expressions as strained as ours must have been last autumn. The ladies totter and have to be steadied, as we were. Then I see a vision so wonderful, so unexpected, joy overcomes all thought. Amelia! My cousin and dearest friend! I cannot restrain myself. Sylvette and I break from the line and run to her. In my happiness I forget to curtsy but instead grip Amelia so hard about the arms she lurches backward, and we both nearly fall atop Sylvette, circling us wildly.

"Eugenie!" she cries. "What manner of greeting is this?"

"The Queen! Have you come with the Queen, Amelia?"

She catches her breath. "*Non.* All winter we have been in Philadelphia. The vicomte found us a dwelling and there we stayed, since we could not travel until now."

"Philadelphia? Have you at least had word of the Queen?"

"We heard that she has escaped the *Conciergerie* and is in hiding somewhere, with Marie-Thérèse and Louis-Charles." Amelia steps farther away from me and regains her dignity.

"And this is certain?" I ask.

"*Non.* But we believe it must be true."

"But Amelia, you do not know it for certain?"

"There was to be a ship waiting offshore, an American

vessel. It was to take them to Southampton, in England, and finally to America. We heard this just before we ourselves left, secretly, of course."

"But Amelia, if you heard of this plan, perhaps so did her captors."

"They are stupid people! They will not have heard."

We stare at one another. I notice how much older she appears. Her beautiful, lion-gold eyes are threaded with red. And under each is a sunken lilac crescent her face powder cannot fill, or mask.

"Eugenie," she says. "What has happened to you? You look . . . completely different."

I brush at my cloak, my hair, and see that I have forgotten to put on my gloves. My hands are red! I do not remember powdering my face today, so that must be red, too.

"I? Well, it is quite an amusing story, Amelia—"

But she has turned from me to stare at our settlement, the few trees mere sticks and the only green that of the pines and hemlocks climbing the hillsides and the steep mountain across the river.

"We are to live *here?*" she says.

"Oh, Amelia, I have much to tell you, and you, me." I link my arm within hers and try not to be sad when she pulls away from me again.

At the riverfront the marquis is speaking with the Vicomte de Noailles, who has also arrived with the flotilla, and then the vicomte tells everyone what Amelia has just told me. Our neat lines dissolve. Workers depart from the landing. Maman and the Comtesse de Sevigny lead Amelia and my aunt Sophie and uncle Chemin to our *petite maison* for Hannah's flummery, cake, and tea. There will have to be another lottery for the newly finished *maisons*. And Papa may soon have need to practice his joinery skill—if, now, Maman allows.

But Amelia! I hold her arm, steadying her as we walk, though I am trembling too. Will Hannah curtsy to Aunt Sophie and Uncle Chemin? Will they like her cuisine? And how scornful will Aunt Sophie be about her own *petite maison?* She is looking with disapproval upon everything as she walks up our avenue. Her tightly closed mouth forms a horseshoe. Upon reaching our *petite maison,* I step up onto the small porch John Kimbrell has built for us and lean to pull off my boots.

"What are you doing, Eugenie?" Aunt Sophie asks with dreadful censure.

"Eugenie!" Amelia adds. "What are those?"

To Maman's exceeding discomfort—and my own— both Aunt Sophie and Amelia study me with intense concentration. It reminds me of Versailles, how we all scrutinized one another, looking for flaws. Aunt Sophie is so beautiful, it has always frightened me to look directly at her, especially when she is looking directly at me. She has a Spaniard's dark hair and brows but fair, luminous skin, and she has always favored brilliant silk gowns to enhance her coloring. Today, her gown is cerise, with matching shoes and a hat with gray feathers. But, really, it is her eyes that unsettle one so. They are gray shading to a hint of blue or silver, depending on the light. With these eyes she regards my boots and then my hot face. I am before a judge never known to pardon anyone.

Attempting a diversion, Maman says, in her brightest tones, "You see what happens in this wilderness? You had best return to Philadelphia at once!"

"One moment, please!" I cry. "You must hear the story of these boots." I begin to tell how the boots were made by the best joiner at the settlement, and how they helped me save Sylvette from the river.

I may as well not have spoken. *"Laid!"* Aunt Sophie pronounces. *Ugly!* As she steps back to get a better look at me—gown, hair, face—her expression says it as well. *Très laid!*

But at least inside our *maison,* Hannah curtsies to each of them and says not a word. Her eyes, though, find mine, and I see fear there. Aunt Sophie ignores her. *Merci, My Lady.* It strikes me that Aunt Sophie is exactly as I was last autumn—incapable of seeing beyond appearances.

By evening my joy at Amelia's arrival has all but eroded when Papa tells us that Monsieur Rouleau, his wife, daughters, and two slaves will depart when the flotilla returns after taking provisions farther upriver.

In a week, perhaps, then.

Soon after dinner, I leave our *maison* on the pretext of giving Sylvette her evening walk and make my way to Hannah's.

Hannah

"Mademoiselle!"

Eugenie puts finger to mouth, hushing me.

Sylvette wishes to get down and sniff at the animals in our shed. I fear a commotion of barking and squawking and who knows what else. I fear John will come in, any moment, and then he does. He stops upon seeing Eugenie standing near Violet's stall—Eugenie in dark cloak, its hood raised. Her face and Sylvette's are as white as John's in the dusk of our shed.

She speaks in short French sentences that John and I do our best to comprehend. Her left hand clutches Sylvette against herself, and her right dances through the air, panto-miming what she is attempting to tell us.

The slaves.

The forest.

The skiff.

The settlement downriver.

On the air she sketches a round shape and then gestures to her own mouth.

Food.

She lifts her cloak and mimics throwing it about herself.

Cloaks.

She points to John and then, with her right hand, makes rowing motions.

John to take them.

She crouches, head lowered.

Hidden. In the skiff.

I look to the door connecting this shed to our cabin and pray that Father will stay inside, near the fire.

Sylvette begins whining.

"Hush, *ma petite!* Hush!"

"Quand?" I ask. When?

She holds up nine fingers. "On the ninth day," she continues in French, "we hide them. Rouleau goes with boats."

I explain to John what I take to be the full meaning of her words. The flotilla arrives in nine days. Early on the day of its arrival, we hide Estelle and Alain until the flotilla must necessarily leave.

"What if the rivermen hold the boats for Rouleau?" John asks. "So he can search?"

"They won't hold the boats, will they, John?"

Uncomprehending, mademoiselle looks from one to the other of us.

"They might," he says. "I wonder if the slaves understand the risk? Can you ask her that?"

I try out several sentences, and Eugenie finally nods. In the next minute she leaves through the shed's pasture door. I sit on the milking stool, my legs no match for the weight of me.

Violet gives a moan, and I stand. John takes the stool and begins the milking while I see to the chickens. What about after the settlement? I ask myself, who will take the slaves farther? Can John? How? Or, can he trust someone else to do that? And where should they go? To our farm? Surely someone will search for them there. Nay. Not our farm, then. But where?

"John, we may have to write a letter they can carry to show folks. A letter telling what they have endured and that they wish, now, to be free. No matter, I think, if we give their names."

"Nay, Hannah. No names. A letter in English, though, 'tis a good idea."

"But if they are sought, there shall be descriptions. And Alain's scars . . ."

"Still, best not to give names."

"Oh, the nobles will suspect us for certain. And what if the flotilla waits and does not leave with Rouleau at once? Waits so that a search . . ."

"Father said 'tis a high wall to scale."

"I know not what to do, John. Now, I mean. Before, it seemed possible."

"Aye." He pauses in the milking. "Maybe I won't use the skiff, Hannah. Just walk them down. Or, better maybe, upriver."

"But thy boot prints."

"Oh. Aye."

"What if they go by themselves? Alain can row, or even Estelle. Then they can keep going as far as they wish."

"But they will be seen on the river and accused of stealing the skiff. Also, they need to be hidden by someone. I may have to go to the settlement first and try to arrange it. And, too, the current flows south, yet they should go north. Into New York, then on to Massachusetts. Or even Canada."

"A terrible hard journey for them. Oh, John, we weave a web to catch ourselves. And maybe them, too."

"But it must be done, aye?"

Before sleep, I go over and over it. And then it is the French Queen I am trying to help escape.

When I open my eyes, I know I have been dreaming.

Eugenie ๛

Amelia and I stand on a small island surrounded by barn-yard puddles as Hannah leads Violet into the shed. Our parasols are raised, our skirts are raised, and so are Amelia's arched eyebrows.

"Do you remember," I say to her, "how Marie Antoinette loved to play at being a shepherdess and how she wore entire pastoral scenes in her hair? Lambs and shepherds with crooks?"

"But this is something else entirely, Eugenie. Sheep muddy to their necks. An odorous cow. To care for animals such as these, one must nearly *be* an animal. Look! A dung pile, right there."

"Amelia. Hannah understands our language."

"What matter if she does? It is the truth, *non?*"

"You insult her."

"I? Insult *her?* All this is an insult to me! I cannot imagine why my parents agreed to this. Or your maman."

It is indeed extraordinary—and all due to Papa. Amelia's parents are so unnerved by this American wilderness, Papa convinced them, as well as Maman, of the necessity to at least become familiar with a few important skills.

After Hannah milks Violet, she asks in French if we would like to watch her make butter.

"Far more preferable to eat it," Amelia says.

To her displeasure, I do not laugh. And to my horror, Hannah replies in French, "Soon you shall, mademoiselle."

Amelia turns to me. "Is this servant in the habit of addressing nobles as her peers, Eugenie?"

My reply lacks grace and wit. "Today . . . well, it is different, today. She is our . . . instructor."

"Yours, perhaps, but not mine. I am here solely for the amusement, poor though it is."

Several hens pecking nearby distract Amelia, and as she shakes her gown at them, I catch Hannah's eye and raise a finger to my lips. Of course she is quick to understand that she must not address Amelia directly again.

In a workroom, Hannah shows us a peculiar object and says in English, "Butter churn."

The apparatus looks like a closed cask with a flat bottom. A pole emerges from its top, and I am thinking of Papa poling the boat here, so long ago, it seems.

"*L'anglais,*" Amelia says, "is the language of our enemy! I shall never speak it."

Why is she being so tiresome and bellicose? It strikes me that she is like Rouleau in a way, taking out on others her own unhappiness.

"Amelia, Amelia, is this not better than endlessly practicing the harpsichord?"

"*Non!* I would rather do anything else in the world than this. *C'est ridicule!*"

I very much doubt that she would rather be in France right now, hiding in some cellar. But I hold my tongue. Hannah is showing us something else. A stone trough of some kind. Into it she pours a pail of milk, waits awhile, and then gestures opening a small drain at the bottom of the trough. Cream, she explains, will rise to the top. Watery milk will drain into another pail. We await this scientific experiment for some time, Amelia curious despite herself.

"Voilà!" Hannah finally says, as she pours thick cream into the churn. She demonstrates raising and lowering the pole, and after a few minutes pauses to gesture to me. I blush, again thinking of Papa on the boat.

"Go ahead, Eugenie," Amelia says. "Follow your heart's deepest desire and become . . . a peasant."

I cannot stay the anger. "Of course you are aware, Amelia, that the Austrians are known for their ruggedness and strength. Marie Antoinette, being of Austrian blood, may well enjoy learning how to churn butter." I say the last two words in emphatic English.

Amelia offers her Versailles laugh, a tinkling chandelier of scorn. "*Pardonnez-moi,* Eugenie, but Marie Antoinette, née Maria Antonia, has journeyed too far from the farms and pastures of Austria to enjoy anything here."

I grip the pole and move it up and down rapidly, as Hannah did. In no time, I am exhausted and must give up. Hannah resumes the work and continues for long minutes.

"This is boring!" Amelia complains. "And I am tired of standing. Imagine! If we did this all day, what time would we have for our amusements?"

These words cause me to view our rank from a new perspective. Before, it meant lands and jewels and court life and privileges. Now I realize it means time itself as well. Because of our servants, we could endlessly dance and visit and amuse ourselves. We had freedom and time, whereas they, in their servitude, had self-sufficiency.

"Amelia, the answer may lie in the golden mean."

"And that is?"

"You must remember from your tutors—Aristotle's golden mean. Moderation. Avoiding extremes."

"Do you *mean* to say, Eugenie, a little bread-baking and a little dancing?"

"Something like that, perhaps, yes."

"It seems a half-baked notion!"

We both laugh at her witticisms, and it feels good to be close again. I so want Amelia to understand, to see what I am beginning to see.

"Amelia, do you not feel unskilled compared to Hannah? And weak?"

"*Non!* And why should I want to do what she does? She is born to do it—not I."

"You miss the point—"

"There is no point! *Écoutez!* Your Papa has become most eccentric, Eugenie. A dangerous development. You must not become like that. Everyone will soon shun you."

Our raised voices cause Hannah to glance at us in fear while she churns the butter. Finally she stops and opens the cask.

We look inside.

Butter. Pale and creamy and thick.

I exclaim in praise, but Amelia is mute. Hannah carries a plate of the fresh butter into the *maison*'s common room and sets it upon the table, along with two cups of cider. Then she takes a loaf of bread from the hearth's warming oven and slices it. In memory, cries of rioting come, and a vision of a mob shoving at bakery doors, smashing windows, grabbing for the few loaves, fighting one another for them.

Hannah, afraid to speak, I realize, motions us to the table. Amelia takes the armchair that must be Monsieur Kimbrell's. I take a plain one that might be Hannah's—or John's. Hannah places buttered bread before each of us. Amelia eats. I cannot.

"What is the matter?" Amelia says.

I shake my head, and then, for Hannah's sake, eat the bread.

It is perfect.

Later, while Hannah shows us how to make bread, Amelia amuses herself by scattering flour everywhere. She even tosses some at me and throws a handful into my hair.

"Amelia, stop!"

"Why?"

She throws some into the air. "Snow, Eugenie!"

The vision of the rioting mob comes again. "You are . . . wasting it."

"Yes—and?"

The flour is silken in my hands. I was enjoying mounding it, kneading it, and told Amelia so. Is this her retaliation?

Flour is everywhere on the floorboards. "I am sorry, Hannah," I say. Kneeling, she is gathering it into a bowl and saying something in French, something about the animals.

"You apologize to a peasant, Eugenie?"

"I"—my voice quakes—"*Oui.*"

"How . . . interesting."

Leaving, Amelia sweeps one hand casually over the table, scattering yet more flour. She allows the *maison*'s door to shut with a great thud and clatter.

"*Pardonnez-moi,*" Hannah says.

"*Moi, aussi.*" The words just there, between us. They seem a gift we give to each other.

Exhausted, I rest while Hannah finishes shaping the dough into loaves. How long it all takes. Then while the loaves rise in a small oven built into the hearth, she begins yet another task—spinning wool into thread.

Watching her, I imagine Papa asking, What do you think is better? Knowing how to make bread or how to play piquet?

The fragrance, now, from Hannah's oven settles the matter.

And yet an idea comes, a wild thought I impulsively voice. "Hannah, would you like to learn to play the harpsichord?" I mime playing a keyboard.

When she fully understands my question, joy brightens her face, but then she shakes her head. "It will not be permitted, mademoiselle."

To my shame, I am relieved. "Ah, well, then." But when she gives me a basket holding three warm loaves, I say something that surprises me as much as it does her.

"Ask your father, Hannah, please."

Returning to our *maison,* I worry that I in fact have become eccentric and that the Queen herself will censure me. Seeing Monsieur Deschamps at work on the Queen's garden, I call good afternoon, more to divert myself. After bowing he asks if I wish to observe how well the lilacs prosper.

Monsieur Deschamps may certainly be described as an eccentric. Upon fleeing France, he brought a barrel containing roots and bulbs and seeds but little else. So now, he must wear the same poor frock coat day after day. Yet his transplanted lilacs are beautifully budding out in chartreuse points that resemble tiny crowns. This makes monsieur all but dance. The canes of his roses, however, have not fared so well. Many appear black and lifeless.

"I shall cut them back but not uproot. *Non.* They may simply need more time to adapt to their new home."

"Monsieur, tell me. Is some of that soil there French soil?"

"Ah, it is! I wanted them to feel at home here."

I kneel and touch the soil of France mingling with American earth, and of course tears come.

"Do not be sad, mademoiselle. All will be well. The Queen will come, and there will be fleur-de-lis and lilacs and roses and herbs for her. You will see!"

"And wonderful *pain,* monsieur. Hannah Kimbrell performs miracles with flour just as you perform miracles here."

"Monsieur Kimbrell does the same with wood. A pity they will not be paid a *sou* for all their work."

"What do you mean? I thought that my father—"

"Pardon me, mademoiselle, but if you do not know."

"Tell me, monsieur!"

"Well. I have heard that the family must give up its wages because the father and the son have not been bowing to the nobles. It is a matter of etiquette, not ability."

"Of course."

The gardener gravely nods. And, as I seem to be controlled by impulses today, I impulsively take one of the loaves from my basket and offer it to him. *"Pour vous,* monsieur! From Hannah Kimbrell."

"Maman, Maman, do you know what I have just heard today, from Monsieur Deschamp?"

"Eugenie, wait. I have something to tell you."

Her expression is so joyful, it can only mean one thing. "The Queen, Maman? She is coming soon?"

"Non. Not that, forgive me. It is . . . You shall have a sister or a brother in September. I wished to be certain before saying anything."

"How wonderful! I hope for a sister! Ah, what a day this

has been, and now we shall celebrate with this wondrous bread your daughter has helped make."

Maman's brightness fades. I deploy an army of words at this sadness. "Should we need bread, Maman, I know how to make it! Is that not all to the good? It is much work but not impossible. We can do it together. The flour, it is so soft!"

"Eugenie, calm yourself. *Mon Dieu.*"

"But you see, Maman, we need not starve. All we need is flour, water, yeast, a bit of salt, an oven, and—voilà! Papa was right. It is good to feel that one can . . . do something that matters."

"Yes, knowledge . . . I suppose, but—"

"And now these Kimbrells, who can do everything—Did you know, Maman, that they will not be paid at all for their work?"

"*Oui.* I knew."

"It is not right. And today Amelia scattered flour all over, to be mean, and Hannah said nothing. She—oh, Maman, are we nobles going to be the same way here in America? Mean to those below us?"

"Eugenie, stop, please. You are talking nonsense."

"But I am not, Maman!"

"*Oui.* You are tired, after your day, and I am, too."

"Oh, Maman. I am sorry. Rest, please. You must. And do not be sad. We have so much, do we not?"

Words startling us both.

"And now, Maman, I have something to beg of you."

❧ Hannah

"The harpsichord?"

"Aye, Father! She would like us to play a simple tune together at the opening of *La Grand Maison*. She will play the harder part. I will merely create the rhythm, she says."

"Daughter, 'tis one thing to learn to play the harpsichord, but quite another to play it before nobles. But first, why does she wish to teach thee?"

I hesitate. Finally I say, "Mademoiselle de La Roque wants to . . . repay me for helping her."

Father looks down at the table. I know he is thinking of how we will earn naught this year.

"And she is so . . . taken with the idea of this *fête*. I think she is just happy and desires everyone to be a part of this happiness, too."

Again I pause but then decide to tell him everything except our escape plan, should our harpsichord plan fail. "And, too, Father, she thinks that Mr. Talon will then help Estelle and Alain if she asks him for that favor." I explain her idea—that on an evening when Father is to be honored for managing the completion of *La Grand Maison*, and when his daughter shows that she can play the harpsichord, Mr. Talon will be in a generous mood. For this is how, she explained, things worked at the Queen's court in France and so will work here, too.

"I doubt, child, that he will be so generous. He seems set hard against any interference."

I have made this very argument to Eugenie and even told her about my futile visit to the marquis. Her response was that at least we must *try*, which is what I now say to Father.

"Dost thou think that thou can learn well enough?" Father asks.

"I believe I can, Father."

I understand why Father asks this question. 'Tis because he believes we must do well whatever we set out to do. That is why he is such a good joiner, and when he farms, a good farmer. It is why most people soon come to respect him.

After a long silence, he says, "Thou may learn to play the harpsichord, Hannah. As for the day of the *fête*, if thou wishes not to play, then I'll not judge thee harshly for declining. Mademoiselle de La Roque may have some success with the nobles on her own."

"I thank thee, Father."

"Good night, now, child. Thou art a treasure. Always remember that I love thee well."

"And I love thee well, Father!"

This wealth of ours, this love, causes me to think about Estelle and Alain. They do not seem in the least joyful. Shunned by the French and ignored by the workers, they are truly orphans. Estelle says little now as she washes clothing. And she is so thin and looks poorly. There is no song in her. She does not smile. Today I found her brushing last autumn's leaves from the graves of her mother and uncle. Father and John and Mr. Stalk dug them as deep as if they were to hold bodies. But the bodies, of course, are not there. Just bits of clothing and a few bones.

"Estelle," I said, "I am sorry." She nodded and lowered her head. Then she braced her forehead with one hand and wept.

"Estelle, remember that Mademoiselle de La Roque has a plan to help you and Alain," I added in French. "Do not weep so, please."

She shook her head and murmured something. I stooped alongside her—she was kneeling on the wet earth, unmindful of her thin gown.

"*Pardonnez-moi,* Estelle, but I did not hear you."

"*Je désire la mort.*"

"Estelle! I do not want you to die," I said carefully in French. "Please do not think thus."

Using sawn tree limbs bound with rope, she and Alain have made two crosses for the graves. There's a white seashell and also a small bowl she fills with pieces of fish and other food when she visits. I do not tell her that animals come in the night and eat it. She probably knows. At that moment the bowl was heaped with slices of dried apple. "Your mama," I said, "wants you to live." I knelt and held her as she went on weeping and trying to say words I took to mean, "But I want to be with her."

I helped her stand and brought her to our cabin. There, she sat close to the hearth and shivered like a lamb born in cruel weather and brought in from the wind and sleet.

Our plan must work.

"*Bon!* You can do it! See? Now, again."

Eugenie plays the melody with her right hand in the

upper keys, and I make a thumping rhythm with my left at the opposite end of the instrument, where the low-sounding keys are. Then I must also play a bit of melody with my left hand, too. For the thumping, my fingers have to stretch far over the keys, back and forth. For the melody, they must play *nine* notes quite nimbly. Eugenie is patient. She waits for me like a bird that can already fly. I am so awkward. "*Pardonnez-moi*, mademoiselle! I cannot."

"Yes, you can, Hannah. Watch."

Thump-thump, thump-thump goes her left hand, then a sprightly tap-tap, tap, tap, tap, tap, tap, tap, tap. She lifts her fingers from the keys and hums the bass melody. I wipe my brow and hands, take a breath, and set shaky fingers on the correct keys for the first thumping notes.

"All right? *Un, deux, trois*—"

We get through two measures and then the hard sprightly part. Eugenie slows her flitting so that I can keep up.

"*Bon! Magnifique*, Hannah!"

We have done four measures, and the next four, she tells me, are exactly the same. So if I can do these four, I can do eight.

When we finally raise our hands from the keys again, even my legs are shaking. Looking at the rest of the notes on the page of music, I can tell that there will be quite a lot of thumping but also more melody, which is harder than the rhythm.

"Mademoiselle, I fear that I cannot—"

"But you can, Hannah. In fact, you are already doing so. Now, again."

This time, I can hear it! *Music.* It fills the cabin, swirls there, tumbles away, and then returns. Like this spring.

It is a work, Eugenie tells me, by a German composer named Johann Sebastian Bach. A simple piece, she says. I say nothing, for I do not wish to be rude. Yet 'tis anything but simple for me. "Musette" is the name of the piece. It means *little music,* she explains. I like the name. It reminds me of *Sylvette.*

Madame de La Roque surprises us both by applauding. When I leave their cabin, I am tired as never before.

Dearest Mother, Grace, Suzanne, and Bonny Richard. 'Tis finally spring here. The days warm. The light strengthens. The river is full and brown and reminds me how, soon, it shall bring us back to thee. How big thou must be, my Richard—near two years old! I can fair see thee, tottering from Grace to Suzanne and back again. Wilt thou remember thy sister Hannah when she returns? Oh, thou must! How I long to hold thee again, wee one. And my dear sisters, thou must be boiling down the sap these warm days. Thy hands sticky with it. My heart hurts to think of thee working so hard and I not there to help. I want so much to be with thee in this springtime. I want so much to share thy work, Mother. To plant the garden with thee. Shear the sheep. Spin our yarn. Tuck wee Richard in and then sing to him. Thou art a tree, Mother, whose strength I dearly miss. And thy wisdom, for trees are wise, are they not? They seem so.

These days the scent of wet earth fills the night. Air and earth are like becoming one! Curious, how the word spring *also means water . . .*

I raise the quill and think how I will miss Jenny, too, when we finally leave. *Jenny*—my secret name for her. A name sweet as her little dog.

Tonight I am naught but longing.

Nay, fears, too. For all of us.

Eugenie

The more closely I look at her, the prettier she becomes. And—now here is the mystery—her plain garb has either nothing or perhaps everything to do with it. Because it does not distract from her face, one focuses on that and gradually comes to see that what appears to be plainness is truly beauty in simplicity, as in our little Bach piece, "Musette." Tonight her unadorned face burns with a lovely inner light. A simple white cap covers her dark hair, her long braid wound up under it. I wish I could paint her portrait in that cap and dark gown. The light of cap and face and collar, the dark of eyebrow and gown. And the only color, a lovely pink blush to her skin. The warmth of *La Grande Maison* gives her face the sheen of a tulip. Certainly all present tonight must notice these attributes. See and be amazed.

But no. Hannah, her equally striking brother, and their father stand unnoticed to one side of the great parlor, while the rest of us float about in our cloudlike gowns, delighted by so much space within which to circle. We resemble boats all festooned, bobbing here and there. Maman is so happy this night! I think we have forgotten how cramped we have been in our little *maisons*—forgotten until tonight. It is almost like being home. Or at least it is not so difficult to imagine being home again. The log walls of *La Grande Maison* have been burnished to the glow of copper pans. There are chairs and tables of cherry wood. Glazing for the windows and brocade draperies. Chandeliers for candles, many candles, the pewter bright as silver. A thick Persian carpet in shades of red, blue, pink, green, and beige. I can almost see Marie Antoinette seated on the tapestry settee, playing cards at one of Monsieur Kimbrell's lovely little tables, while breezes flow in through the tall open doors.

Ah! The Comtesse de Sevigny signals that it is time for the music. The early program will be informal. We lesser musicians are to play while people continue to chatter or listen, as they please. *Bon*. That will be better for Hannah. After supper will come the formal program, during which the true musicians will play. The Marquis de Talon, our dear abbé, the Comtesse de Sevigny, and Monsieur Ridenour, who was choirmaster in the chapel at Versailles. Then after those performances, dancing.

"Amelia," I say. "It is time. Do you wish to play first?"

"Are you truly going to play with your servant?"

"If Hannah so wishes."

"Why do you persist in wanting to do that? If she makes a mistake, as she no doubt will, and you have to start over, everyone will laugh."

"She will not make any mistakes, Amelia."

"How can you be so certain?"

"She knows the piece well. Also, everyone is engaged in conversation. They will neither notice nor laugh if there should be a small mistake."

"Of course they will laugh. Besides, is it not like asking your Sylvette to walk on her hind legs?"

"That is a mean thing to say. Are you so jealous of Hannah, Amelia?"

"*Non!* But you are being foolish. She can never fit in with us."

"You are wrong, cousin. She already has."

"The Queen will not approve, Eugenie."

"I believe that Marie Antoinette, were she here, would indeed approve—and applaud us. She has an eye for beauty and Hannah is beautiful. She appreciates courage and Hannah is courageous. She values accomplishment and Hannah is accomplished, in her own way."

"A mere servant!"

"*Non!* An American."

"Go then. Your *Américaine* awaits you."

Amelia, jealous. Why? I am to play a duet with her as well, a far more complicated piece. When one is jealous, one is usually afraid. What could Amelia possibly be afraid of? She is still my cousin, still my dear friend, though not so dear at this moment. In fact, her jealousy makes her most unattractive. A scowl and furrows—when she should be joyful. A *brillant* flower, not a mule!

I am detained by Comtesse de Sevigny, and when I turn, I see that Amelia is curtsying before Hannah and saying something. Fear steals my breath as I move toward them, hampered at every step by hoop skirts.

Hannah

"Ah, *ma petite!*" Amelia says. "*C'est ton grand début, non? Bonne chance!*" Then she turns to face the nobles. "*Écoutez, écoutez!*" she calls out. It means *listen*. But after that I know not what she's saying, for she speaks too fast until the words, "*Oui! L'artiste! Très bonne!*"

She's telling them that I am an artist! A very good artist. Why does she do this?

The nobles are applauding now, and every eye seems fixed upon me. My hands and face, my whole body stiffens. The rug's fanciful shapes rise up and appear large, surrounding me.

Someone pulls me forward. Amelia. Urging me toward the harpsichord.

"*Non,*" I say. "*S'il vous plaît! Excusez-moi!*"

Then Eugenie appears at my side and takes my other arm. She raises her voice and speaks to the gathering, but I do not understand these words either. I give both arms a downward tug and free myself of the two. The quiet is frightening as I walk back to Father and John.

"Father, please remain, for they have invited thee and John, but I wish to go back to the cabin."

"I will walk with thee."

"Please stay, thou and John. It may appear disrespectful."

But John takes my arm and soon we're outside in the cool spring evening, with Father. Robins are chirping. The watery scent of the earth is strong. From behind us comes the sound of the harpsichord. Perhaps it is Eugenie, playing our piece by herself. But no, 'tis not "Musette." Rather, something much harder.

"Art thou very disappointed?" John asks.

"Aye," I say, after a while. "I do not understand why Amelia would do such a thing."

Father walks a few paces before saying, "It may be because she wants her cousin to herself."

"But Eugenie loves her as a sister."

"For some people 'tis not enough."

John picks up a stone and heaves it into a rough plot that one day might be someone's yard. I feel less cold now though very tired and hungry. All the cooking I did today has been for the *fête.*

"Father," I say, "please return with John. At least have thy supper there. Let them see that it is no great matter, for truly 'tis not."

"Then perhaps thou should return with us?"

I understand his reasoning, and something in me urges, *Do it for Estelle.* Yet my limbs go weak at the thought of re-entering *La Grande Maison.*

"I am sorry, Father, but I cannot. It would please me much, though, if thou and John were to return. There is but bread and cheese at home."

"And tea?" he asks.

"And tea."

"And a bit of applesauce, perchance?" John says.

"Yes, some applesauce," I say, lighter of heart for their teasing.

"Well, that sounds fine!"

As I'm setting the table, we hear a soft knock upon our door.

Eugenie. With her hair all white and piled high, she looks like a queen. Her face is a snowfield under the sun, her gown a blue I could not have imagined before —lighter, greener than the sky's blue, with red roses cascading down from shoulder to hem. At *La Grande Maison* she blended in with the rainbow of ladies there, but here in our cabin, she is the sun itself.

Finally, I can speak. "Thou bringest *La Grand Maison* to us!"

John and Father have gone stone quiet. I say in French, "Will you have some tea?"

"Of course! *Merci!*"

John and Father stood when she entered. Now John slides one of our chairs out far from the table to accommodate Eugenie and her gown. His hands seem fixed to the chair back.

"John," I whisper. "John!"—breaking his trance.

Eugenie seats herself slowly but pretends not to notice how long it all takes. Finally she says in slow French, "I wish to tell you how much I regret such inexcusable behavior." She gives me a piercing look that conveys her deeper meaning: *Do not allow her to spoil our plan.*

"*Merci,* mademoiselle." I set a plate of cheese upon the table. I slice bread. I set out mugs for us.

She eats some of the bread and cheese and applesauce.

"Thou wilt spoil thy appetite for the feast," I say. The thought of Jenny here on such a night brings tears I blink away.

"Ah, *non!* This makes a delicious first course!"

"You should return soon," I say in French. "They will soon miss thee."

"And they will miss you also."

Her eyes are full upon me, and I fully understand her meaning.

Father says in French, "Hannah wishes us to return without her."

"And you, John?" Eugenie asks in French and laughs.

John regards the table as if it were some valuable. "I believe . . . Well, it was quite . . ." In his panic, he can utter only English.

I know he felt as out of place as I, there, but I say, "John did not wish to leave, Eugenie. He did so for me."

Eugenie is almost too bright. Like John, I want to keep my eyes lowered.

"Hannah," Eugenie says quietly, with no trace of teasing, "please return. You need not play. Come for the supper, please, and to hear the others perform. It will be most beautiful." This she says half in French and half in English. "And then," she adds, "there may be some . . . speeches of interest."

Her meaning is clear.

"Please, Hannah? Be courageous, no?"

Courage. The word is the same in both languages despite the different pronunciation.

I tell myself that I should have just laughed when Amelia said those things. Or simply smiled and then gone on to do what we'd intended. Now I see it clearly: my pride is standing in the way of our helping Estelle and Alain. My fear that the nobles think that I believe myself to be a musician.

So much worry to so little end.

"It is not too late?" I ask.

"Not if we go quickly!"

Father and John follow as Eugenie and I walk side by side under the stars, back to *La Grand Maison*. It is quite dark, with no moon. She was brave to come—alone!—to our cabin. Can I do any less?

My throat feels swollen, my hands are stiff with cold. How shall I move my fingers over the keys? And when I open my mouth to speak, will any sound at all come out?

But Eugenie takes my arm as we walk together toward the lighted house.

Then, somehow, I am stepping toward the instrument placed in a corner of a fancy room. I am seating myself alongside Eugenie at the keyboard. She glances at me and whispers, *"Un, deux, trois."*

And then we are playing.

I try to think only of the notes. I do not even hear the music. Soon 'tis over and we are raising our hands from the keyboard. Eugenie smiles at me and whispers, *"Bon,* Hannah!" She pushes back her chair and stands, and so do I. My chair does not tumble backward. Both of us curtsy to the nobles.

"Mes amis," Eugenie begins in French. "Honorable nobles of the French court, Hannah Kimbrell, who has just played so delightfully, wishes to address us tonight and begs your permission to do so. I ask you, please, to grant it and to listen closely to what she has to say. I shall translate where necessary."

At least this is what she told me earlier, in simple French, that she would say. Now the words shake me to the bones. There are murmurs followed by an awful silence. I am not

about to speak to Marie Antoinette's nobles, am I? I fear
they all can see my mouth trembling, and my jaw with it.
But the thought of Estelle at the grave steadies me.

"Thank you," I begin in French. A bit of light appears
like a widening circle, and I can see Madame d'Aversille,
her wrinkly face snowy with powder. Her eyebrows are
raised halfway up her forehead. Her mouth tugs upward.
The wrinkles follow like ripples. She is smiling!

"It is good of you . . ." But all the French words I practiced as hard as I had practiced the piece with Eugenie
scatter from my mind.

"English, Hannah," Eugenie whispers.

After drawing a breath, I go on in simple French. I tell
how I came upon Estelle at the graves. How thin and weak
she is, and sad. How she has lost everything in this world
but her brother and her memories of her family. "You all
have lost much as well, but yet you hope for a return to your
old life. Estelle has no such hope. Could you find a way to
free her and her brother and offer them sanctuary here?
A sanctuary as you yourselves have? They did nothing to
deserve their fate. And they have much to offer the settlement. Estelle is a very good cook. Abbé La Barre can get
a book about the cheeses you enjoyed in France. You can
have a creamery here, with Estelle and Alain in charge of it.
Together, you can purchase goats and milk cows and have
cheese for yourselves and to sell."

I want to say much more but my throat swells shut.
"Pardonnez-moi," I can only whisper. *"Merci."*

The room grows murky, and I want to run from it. But
someone begins speaking in French I cannot understand
except for the words *John Kimbrell.*

I fear more punishments shall be heaped upon us.

The vicomte steps forward. In his wig he looks like a judge. I lower my eyes as he nears but for Father's sake do not curtsy again.

The vicomte takes my right hand and says in English, "Hannah Kimbrell, you are a brave girl and your idea is a good one. We regret, however, that we cannot interfere in the matter of Monsieur Rouleau's slaves. We have decided, however, that because of your father and brother's great efforts on our behalf, as well as their excellent workmanship, we shall restore all your family's earnings, even as we respect your right to your beliefs. *Merci*, mademoiselle, for your excellent performance tonight. We had no idea that, in addition to all your other skills, you possess musical ability. And *courage* too!"

He bows and steps back. I hear clapping, but it seems a distance away.

I look to Father and John. John smiles a bit, then goes crimson. I look at Eugenie. She is smiling at him.

And I am seeing our farm, right there amid the nobles in the bright parlor. This joy fades, though, when I remember Estelle at the gravesite.

Eugenie takes my arm and leads me back to Father and John. To Father, she curtsies and says, "*Merci*, Monsieur Kimbrell, *pour tout*. And to you, John."

John closes his eyes, and I fear he may topple over.

"What you have done, ladies, was most brave," Father tells us both.

"But we failed," I say.

"Nay. You tried. Trying is never failure. Only a beginning."

Then someone announces that it is time for dinner, and

to my astonishment—nay, shock!—Eugenie takes John's arm and leads him into the dining room. Several nobles stare, and among them, Florentine du Vallier. A chill passes over me.

I cannot eat much but try so as not to offend. The nobles seem to have forgotten about us. They talk and laugh, and it begins to sound like our "Musette," something large made of many small parts in the way an oak has leaves and stems and the leaves, veins, and rippled bark and limbs like separate trees, and branches filling the sky and inside the branches, sap, and under the earth, branches of roots, and everything connecting, even limbs and sky.

That is us, Hannah, I hear Mother saying. Her voice is so clear, she might be right next to me.

All of us together.

1794

Avril / April

Eugenie ❧

Lovely warmth today but the wind—*Mon Dieu!* It shakes the budding trees as if to break them. Along the clearing, some small yellow flowers are blooming, pipelike things on stems with no leaves to speak of. I did not see them here yesterday. They must have sprouted and bloomed overnight, like mushrooms. I do not quite like them, despite their bright coronas. But all the same, I pick a few.

"Come, Sylvette! Monsieur Deschamps may know what these are called." As we turn toward *La Grande Maison*, where the gardener is sure to be working, I hear wolves howling. This is most unusual, to hear them during the day. But at least they are across the river. "Sylvette. Stay close."

In the lee of *La Grande Maison*, the air holds a fragrance.

"*Bonjour*, monsieur."

"Ah, mademoiselle! *Bonjour!* I must show you something. Look."

I do not know what I am looking at except that it is green and emerging from dark, heaped-up soil.

"Lilies!"

"The Queen, monsieur, will be ecstatic."

"Do you think so?"

"But of course!"

He regards the garden a moment. "So much remains to do. But the soil here is good. I will work wonders."

"Already you have, monsieur. But can you tell me what this little flower might be?"

He takes one and peers at it, turning it this way and that. Then he smells it. "This, I do not know. A weed of some kind, perhaps. An American wildflower."

"Look how they already wilt. Strange things."

"But everything has its place and reason, mademoiselle, in the garden of this world." He hands the limp flower back to me. There is sadness in his voice.

"Indeed, monsieur," I say to be polite. "You are most wise in addition to most skilled."

"*Merci,* mademoiselle."

Not wanting to drop the wilted flowers on Monsieur Deschamp's orderly garden, I carry them away with me.

I wonder if monsieur was thinking of the revolutionists. In America the rebels' purpose was to bring about a new government, a democracy. So then, in France, also? And if a democracy in France, then I . . . will be nothing.

Non! The Queen will come! There will *not* be a democracy for us. We *shall* have our monarchy.

I toss the wilted flowers to the side. "Sylvette, the river! Let us look for a flotilla."

Passing the settlement, the river flows eastward and then loops to the west before turning southward again. One cannot see down its length for any great distance, and except for the curling brown current, it seems more like a lake. In the shallows on the other side, a blue heron stands as still as a branch. On both sides of the river, budding trees wear shawls of fine green lace.

Today the water is all sequins, but again the river is empty. "She will come, Sylvette. Perhaps not today, though."

Sylvette and I turn from the river and walk along the eastern edge of the clearing. As we near the overland trail to Philadelphia, Sylvette begins barking.

Amid the greenery, some dark shape is approaching. I step back but Sylvette remains there, barking and growling. "Come, Sylvette."

"Mademoiselle!" Comte de Sevigny is hurrying toward us. "This way!"

Stooping, I gather up Sylvette. Others, too, have evidently heard Sylvette: the Aversilles, each with a walking stick, and Abbé La Barre, approaching rapidly.

The beast we feared is but a horse and its rider. A post rider—the first since last autumn. Perhaps with word of the Queen!

The rider dismounts and removes his wide-brimmed hat. Then he stands with it over his chest after bowing to us, Sylvette is finally quiet.

"He is showing reverence, that is all," I whisper. But my hands have gone cold.

"What is it?" Sevigny says in French. "Tell us!"

Abbé La Barre goes to the rider and inclines his head as if listening to the man's confession. After a moment the abbé makes the sign of the cross and turns to us.

I am trembling so, and my eyesight seems to be dimming. Someone takes my arm, steadying me, as the abbé says, "The Queen is dead. God rest her soul. Long live our new King, Louis-Charles!"

We kneel on the earth and make the sign of the cross. In the dark chamber of me, I hear the rest of the abbé's words. The plot to free our Queen was uncovered by her captors. The fishing vessel awaiting her off the coast of France had finally sailed without her to England and then back to America. Marie Antoinette went to her death at the guillotine with great dignity and peace and died there on October 16. Her daughter, Marie-Thérèse, has been traded to Austria in exchange for French prisoners of war. Louis-Charles, the titular King of France, remains imprisoned. Word of all this has only recently arrived in America.

We continue kneeling while the abbé leads us in prayers, after which there are cries for further details.

This I cannot bear. I stand and shake my head to clear away the darkness. In the next moment Sylvette and I are running to our *maison*, where Maman is just waking from her nap.

"Maman, the Queen—"

Is dead. But I cannot utter these words. I cannot accept them. Perhaps she escaped afterward, somehow, and news of *that* hasn't yet reached America.

"Eugenie, what has happened?"

Papa throws open the door.

"Papa, is it true?"

"Philippe," Maman says. "What is it?"

He sits alongside her. I go to his other side. "My dears," he says. "I fear it is so. The Queen . . . no longer lives."

Through the open door, I see Florentine passing. He is not walking so much as stumbling forward.

Soon we hear a shot fired, and Papa rushes to learn what it means. When he returns, he is ashen. "Sevigny," he says. "The man has been wounded. Florentine was waving one of his pistols about, threatening to shoot himself. Sevigny tried to get it from him and was shot. A serious wound. I am going to find Hannah. She may be able to help. Eugenie, take care of your mother."

I can only hold her, she is weeping so. An image of the dreaded Blade of Eternity comes, that terrible angled blade. And there is our Queen, kneeling beneath it. I take Maman's hand and hold onto it. Sylvette jumps to my lap and settles herself. We sit here a long while, holding one another. Outside, the spring wind makes its rushing-water sound. Then Maman lies back, and I cover her and rub her forehead. But the pain is not just there, I know. As with me, it is deep, it is everywhere.

I kneel by Maman's bed, my head upon her pillow, and close my eyes. The ache is a river, carrying me I know not where until I hear Hannah whispering, "Eugenie, Eugenie, the flotilla from upstream. It arrives."

Awareness comes pouring back into me. *Not the Queen's flotilla. Our Queen is dead.*

It seems some terrible *knowing*. A terrible power wrapping me around.

Hannah

At her canvas-covered window, I softly call Estelle's name and then walk to a white pine at the edge of the forest. Soon, three figures approach, each in a dark cloak.

Patches of old snow give enough light, with the help of the setting moon. We can see one another well enough. "Come," I say in French, but Estelle shakes her head. I turn to Eugenie. Did she explain everything? How we will hide them in the forest until well after the flotilla leaves, later this morning, with the Rouleau family? How John will get them to a Mr. Banin, from the settlement to the south of us, and Mr. Banin will take them east in his wagon and then arrange for other transport?

"Please," I whisper in French. "Fear not." Estelle and Alain are at least dressed for travel. I give Estelle the bundle I've prepared. "For your journey," I say. I try to place it in her hands. Finally she holds onto it as if it were only more clothing to wash. "Come, Estelle! We must leave now."

John and I walk toward the forest, but the others do not follow. We go back.

"Estelle fears Rouleau too much," Eugenie whispers. "His punishments are *très severe*. Alain is willing but not without Estelle. All night he has tried to convince her."

My own fear deepens. They might be well hidden by now. "Please," I say again in French. "Come with me, Estelle." I tug on her arm, but she pulls back. "Estelle, please. It will be far better for you both. Tell them, mademoiselle."

"I have," Eugenie whispers.

"There!" someone shouts. "There they are!"

A torch suddenly flares orange. I again pull at Estelle's arm, but she drops to her knees and hides her face. Alain crouches alongside her. They look like two stones. Eugenie, John, and I step forward as Mr. Rouleau and Florentine du Vallier appear. The younger man has a coil of rope over his shoulder, and Mr. Rouleau, a drawn pistol. I dare not look toward Estelle and Alain in hope that they will not be seen, there in the shadow at the rim of torchlight.

Foolish hope.

Eugenie says something sharp that causes the young Frenchman to smile meanly. Mr. Rouleau gives him the pistol and strides over to the two dark shapes. Before John can stop him, he kicks one. Alain utters a cry and falls forward. Mr. Rouleau shoves John down as well. John will not fight back though he does try to rise. But Mr. Rouleau has the rope about him and binds his wrists, then Alain's, and finally Estelle's. They are all attached by the same rope. Eugenie's words are a storm I fear will only worsen all this.

Slowly I back away.

"Halt!" Mr. Rouleau shouts in French. "You, too, must pay for this, Mademoiselle Kimbrell." When he turns to Florentine and asks for something to bind me—the rope is all used—I pick up a stone and hurl it into the forest. It clatters against a tree.

"Halt!" Mr. Rouleau shouts again, looking in that direction. "Come here at once or I fire!"

I ease myself backward, a step at a time and soon am moving swiftly away through thick forest. But then shot strikes trees all around serving to make me run faster. Branches slap my face. I slip on stones and fallen trees.

Father is outside our cabin. "Hannah! Where hast thou been? What is this shooting?"

"Oh, Father, thou weren't to know, but it has gone wrong." My throat tightens shut.

"Hannah, quickly—tell me."

I am shaking so, my teeth clatter. "The slaves . . . we tried to help . . . And John . . . he's . . . Mr. Rouleau has them all tied."

"Go inside and bar the door."

Father begins running straight across the clearing. I am running again, too, following him.

Eugenie ❧

"So you have been spying," I cry. "Villain! Rouleau, *gross;* you, *petit,* his shadow, his puppet. Is this how you find your entertainment? Then I am sorry for you, Florentine. You may have noble blood, but it means nothing at all. You may as well be the most ruthless of peasants. Unbind those three at once and redeem yourself."

"Spying, mademoiselle?" Rouleau says. "We had no need of spying. We suspected from the start that you and your Americans would try something like this. As for noble blood, you yourself are the criminal here. The young man is on the side of right. You should be begging his pardon—and mine—for such insults. I shall see that you are made to pay for your villainy, mademoiselle. Aiding runaway slaves is no small offense."

"We were urging them to do so. They, however, did not wish to leave you."

"Ha! A fancy story! Why are they in cloaks, with food in a bundle? And a letter in English! Why are they here, outside their cabin, if they did not intend to leave? They have left already, as you can see for yourself. You were urging them? Well, that adds to the charge. You, too, must be punished, but I suppose they will not because of your so-called noble blood. Still, you shall pay. I demand my rights. I shall demand this of the vicomte."

"And I shall tell the vicomte of your ruthlessness."

"Of course. And he shall listen to one who disdains the law. Allow us to pass or I shall be compelled to fire my weapon again. The boats await us."

I cannot bear to look at Estelle and Alain and John.

Rouleau leads the three toward his *maison*, while Florentine walks ahead with the torch. Then Monsieur Kimbrell and Hannah appear. In the near distance are Maman and Papa, Sylvette racing alongside.

"Eugenie!" Papa cries. "Why are you here? What has happened? We heard shooting." Maman and Papa have thrown cloaks over their dressing gowns and hurry toward me.

"Monsieur Rouleau is going to whip his slaves—or worse. Summon Noailles, Papa. Sylvette, come!" I lift her up and run past Maman and Papa.

Glancing back, I see them turn to follow me.

"The vicomte, Papa!"

"Stay, then, in the *maison*."

Papa hurries toward Talon's *maison*, but Maman is returning to ours.

I carry Sylvette inside and rush to the barrel nearest the wall. The cloth sack is halfway down, hidden under a crinoline. Closing the door upon Sylvette, I am again out on the avenue. Running, I pass Maman.

"Eugenie, what are you doing? Do not go back there, I beg you."

"I must help them."

"He is dangerous!"

But I do not stop. Pushing my way through gathering workers and rivermen, I shout, "Monsieur Rouleau! Might I speak with you a moment?"

"You already have, and in quite a charming manner."

"This time truly speak."

He is still holding his pistol. Hannah stands in front of Estelle, shielding her. Workers have gathered around Monsieur Kimbrell.

"Eugenie!" Maman calls. "Come to me at once!"

"You should obey, mademoiselle," Florentine says.

I am gratified to see that he looks frightened. But I am frightened as well. *Our Lady, help me.*

"Monsieur Rouleau," I say. "I request that you place these prisoners in my care." My voice quavers. I hope it sounds like indignation.

"You need slaves, mademoiselle? Well, this one, as you see, is damaged. He strikes Alain on the face. "And this one . . ." He steps toward John.

"Monsieur Rouleau. Strike anyone again and you shall lose an opportunity you will bitterly regret." I hold the necklace up for him to see in the growing light.

"Eugenie!" Maman calls. *"Mon Dieu!"*

I turn. Sylvette is running toward us. She must have pushed open the door. As she flies at Rouleau, he kicks her aside. She rolls away, yelping in pain. John looks down but cannot help her. Nor I.

"Monsieur," I say. "Restrain yourself or . . . lose this." Diamonds and sapphires dangle from my fingers. "The stones have been set by the eminent goldsmith François-Thomas Germain."

"Eugenie!" Maman cries out again.

"Take it, monsieur. Quickly. Only you must then go to Abbé La Barre and sign your name to a statement declaring that each of the slaves is free forever and that Kimbrell is free of any charge against him."

Rouleau extends his hand. "*Imbécile.* Idiot!"

Closing my eyes, I release hold of Grand-mère's tear-drop diamonds, the pretty gold links of chain, the sea-blue sapphires.

Rouleau turns to the rivermen. "I wish to leave at once. Ready the boats."

Not one of the rivermen moves.

"I command you!"

They stand there, staring at Rouleau.

"Vicomte de Noailles," Rouleau calls as the vicount and Papa rush toward us. "Order these men to ready the boats for us. *This* one, I demand you punish." He takes out a knife and slashes at the rope holding John to Estelle and Alain. Then he pushes John aside.

The vicomte's face is calm. He regards Rouleau for a long moment. "You may neither command nor order any man here," he says finally. "The boats shall leave when I declare they shall."

"Noailles, you're—"

"Refrain from continuing, monsieur."

Abbé La Barre appears with a lap desk, but Maman cries, "*Non, non!* Vicomte, you must not allow this!"

The vicomte addresses me. "Mademoiselle, is that your necklace?"

"It . . . was."

"You do not value it?"

"I do. But I also value their lives. They must be free of Monsieur Rouleau. He has done terrible things. He did not take care of them, and they became ill. When their mother and uncle died, he did not bury them, and wild animals ate the remains. He is a disgrace to this settlement. I tell the truth. Anyone here shall tell you the same."

Monsieur Deschamps approaches the vicomte and offers a deep bow.

"You may speak," the vicomte says.

"Your Excellency, it is true. And I have seen Monsieur Rouleau beating the young man. He had dropped a piece of firewood, and it narrowly missed monsieur's foot. Monsieur then struck the young man a number of times with a large stick."

"And he threw Estelle's boots into the river," I say, "because the Kimbrells made them for her. She has worn only rags on her feet all this past year."

"Talon," the vicomte says. "Can you verify these charges?"

"It is true about the remains. I know not about the firewood incident or the boots, but I assume that neither Monsieur Deschamps nor Mademoiselle de La Roque has any reason to lie."

The vicomte regards the ground. When he looks up and speaks, his voice is quiet. "Why did you not tell me of all this?"

"I myself spoke to Monsieur Rouleau after the deaths. He gave me his word that the remaining two slaves would have provisions and everything necessary."

"*Oui,*" Papa says. "And that was because we all voted on what he must do."

"But you did not tell me about any of it?" the vicomte asks Talon.

Talon says nothing, and the vicomte becomes thoughtful again. Finally he addresses Papa. "Comte de La Roque. You shall lose this necklace forever. What do you want me to do?"

Papa looks at me and then at the vicomte. "I humbly request that you honor my daughter's wish."

"Philippe, *non!*" Maman takes hold of his arm.

The vicomte turns to Abbé La Barre. "Allow Monsieur Rouleau to sign the paper."

The abbé holds the desk out for Rouleau. Rouleau glances at Grand-mère's necklace before scribbling his name on the sheet of foolscap. Then he throws the quill to the ground. Protecting the paper, the abbé steps away from Rouleau. Maman is crying.

"Madame," the vicomte says. "I am sorry for your distress." Then he turns away from her. "Put the Rouleau family on one of the boats immediately," he says, "with all their possessions except those two, who are no longer slaves but free citizens of France. Unbind the American. As the representative of King Louis XVII, I declare it. So be it."

John and Hannah come to my side, John carrying Sylvette, while Papa tries to comfort Maman. The day's new light dims. I mean to take Sylvette from John but instead grip his arm as I sway forward. Vaguely, I sense Hannah holding my other arm. Somewhere in the distance Florentine is challenging John to a duel, in French. Then I am seeing that fire again, engulfing my Annette, a roil of fire-cloud that swiftly burns everything dark.

I awake in my bed, the curtain open. Maman lies in her bed, Papa sitting alongside it, one hand holding his forehead.

"Papa, how is Maman?"

He merely nods.

"What is the hour?"

He raises five fingers. "In the afternoon."

I close my eyes again. *Five.*

"Papa, I must go to Hannah and Monsieur Kimbrell. Permit this, please."

Again he gestures listlessly. Do as you please, he seems to say. What matter, now.

"Papa, it is not Hannah's fault. It was my idea. Let any blame fall upon me, not upon her or Monsieur Kimbrell or John."

"*Oui, oui.*"

There is no one at Hannah's *maison*. The joiners must still be working. As for Hannah, she could be anywhere. I walk to another large *maison* being built near *La Grande Maison*. Yes, workers are there. It surprises me to see Alain among them, on a ladder placed against a chimney. He is handing a stone to someone standing on the roof. A platform is braced against the roof and upon it are other stones, a bucket, and tools. The person on the roof kneels and positions the stone on the chimney, removes it, chips at it with a tool, and replaces it. When he takes off his hat to wipe his brow, I see that he is John Kimbrell *fils*. And approaching just now is Florentine, a wooden case under his left arm.

"Ah! The fair lady observes her prince."

This time I make no retort, not wanting to goad him. "Florentine, he did not understand you. Why not leave? If you persist and he is killed, they will send you and your family away. Your pistols have already done enough damage."

He winces. "They will not send me away! It is a point of honor."

I am nearly too fatigued to go on but force myself to continue. "Florentine, only Hannah heard you. I doubt that she understood your meaning."

"But you did, mademoiselle. And you are the one who

acted so stupidly, throwing away that necklace for slaves. And you did it because of him."

"Then perhaps you should duel me."

"Perhaps I should, but that would be most ungallant, would it not? Therefore, Kimbrell must duel."

"My lady," Alain says, after bowing. "Allow me, please, to take Monsieur Kimbrell's place."

I had not noticed Alain's approach. I raise one hand. "Florentine, they will indeed force you to leave. The marquis and the vicomte will see to it."

"Not over a mere slave."

"But he is no longer a slave. He is a free citizen of France. You heard the vicomte. Florentine, you are brave and you fully understand honor, but here in America there is a law prohibiting duels. Papa has been making a study."

"I do not believe you, mademoiselle."

"Then you risk imprisonment or even . . ." I pause in my fabrication, gratified to see the oily tracks on Florentine's face. ". . . Execution!"

"Compared to a nobleman, he is nothing."

"Here, murder is murder. But perhaps you are right. Given your nobility, the authorities may simply choose to send you back to France. Alone."

An *odeur* rises off Florentine now. Sour. Like spoiled fish.

"A fate perhaps worse than execution," I continue. "We find this law ludicrous, but there it is. So perhaps it is best to forget this matter as no one heard you but the Kimbrells."

"*He* knows. This so-called free citizen."

I turn to Alain. "Monsieur, did you hear Du Vallier challenge anyone?"

Alain finally raises his head. "I was . . . mistaken."

215

"Bah! Here, villain. Defend that other villain!"

Florentine pushes the open pistol box toward Alain. Alain hesitates, and in that pause, I take up one of the pistols and cock it.

"Mademoiselle is brave!" Florentine cries.

He is wincing again. With outstretched arm, I aim directly at his narrow chest.

"Wait, wait! I cannot—no! Give me the pistol, mademoiselle. Give it to me!"

I do not lower it.

"Mademoiselle! *S'il vous plaît.* I cannot . . . shoot you."

"Then I shall have to shoot *you.*" I look directly into his eyes. My hand shakes with some awful anger.

"Mademoiselle, do not fire, I beg you."

His voice quavers like that of a distraught child. I lower the pistol and discharge its ball into the earth.

Florentine steps forward and pulls the pistol from my hand. His pimples gleam.

"You surprise me, mademoiselle, truly." He offers a stiff bow.

Then John and Alain are at my side. Florentine walks off, his box of pistols under his arm. I can tell by his shoulders that he is unsuccessful in his attempt not to cry.

"I need to sit," I say in French.

They lead me to a pile of stones and there I rest, seated upon a large stone. After some time, I no longer tremble. The late-afternoon sun is warm on my shoulders and arms. The scent of newly sawn pine, sweet.

Hannah

Tonight I know not how to ask for guidance. What we have done was wrong, yet also right. All has been gained, and all has been lost. Any possible friendship with Eugenie. Eugenie's necklace. The good will between our families. This evening Madame de La Roque would not even look at me when I brought their meal. Her anger filled the cabin.

Into my thoughts comes a verse from the little counting song Madame d'Aversille so loves.

Over in the meadow in a new little hive, lived an old mother Queen bee and her honey bees five. "Hum," said the mother. "We hum," said the five. So they hummed and were glad in their new little hive.

Tonight Madame d'Aversille hummed the melody as if she were one of the little bees, and for a time I forgot my own misery. Now here it is again.

At the knock upon our door, Father rises.

'Tis the vicomte.

Father invites him to enter and sit near the hearth, in the armchair. But the vicomte stops just within the door. In high-crowned hat and flowing wig and purple cloak, he is a frightening figure. I rise and grip my hands before me. John has risen, too. Father backs away from the vicomte, and the three of us stand facing him.

In English he tells us that we must leave the settlement as soon as another flotilla passes. As for our restored earnings this year, the money will be given to the La Roque family in recompense, however inadequate, for the loss of their irreplaceable family heirloom.

He turns and leaves. We stand there until he is out of view. "Father," I whisper after closing the door. "Forgive us."

"There is naught to forgive. Thou and John and Mademoiselle de La Roque have found a way to free two slaves. 'Tis a great thing, Hannah."

"But our earnings! And our farm!"

Father places a hand on my shoulder. "Your mother will understand, child, as I do. 'Tis our teachings, you know, bearing fruit. Hush now. All will be well."

As we sit at our table in the quiet, the day's events rush though me like dreams. Rouleau's coil of rope, his pistol. The dark capes. The shots. Eugenie's necklace. Sylvette yelping. The quill pen on the ground. The vicomte there in our doorway.

'Tis like falling in brambles, and thorny canes scraping arms, legs, face.

Heart, too.

But finally the images tire of me and there is only the sound of our fire on the hearth, and the stillness holding it. Then comes a small quiet thought. No one died this day, and Estelle and Alain are free.

Eugenie ⟳

"Throw those boots away! She must wash your stockings again. I shall not have the stench of that American leather upon them. Wear your own *souliers.*"

"But Maman, it is so muddy now, with this rain, my *souliers* shall be completely ruined."

"Then do not walk about so. When the Queen—ah, what do I say!"

Maman's brow furrows, her eyes fill, but she collects herself as if from some near fall. "We must show our new King that we have not forgotten who we are, in this wilderness. When the girl arrives, tell her we need more hot water."

The girl. She. Maman refuses to say Hannah's name, nor will she allow Papa or I to do so. She is still so angry about the necklace. *Clean that grate and then wash mademoiselle's stockings—the dirt still shows! And when you have finished, you must sweep the floor again. You have brought in mud!*

Maman eats Hannah's delicious food willingly enough and then, immediately afterward, is so terribly mean. I am ashamed to even think it, but she reminds me, now, of Rouleau. Poor Hannah accepts it all and goes about her work with her usual grace. When she leaves, Maman cries that I have broken her heart—the precious necklace once worn at the courts of three kings, gone forever! "Of all the losses, this is the worst—no, not the worst, but you understand my meaning—and for what, Eugenie? For what? Can you tell me?" Then, when I try yet again to explain, she says that I have lost even the essence of who I am. Throwing away the necklace is proof of this.

"Maman, I at least can fill the pot with water and swing it over the fire. Allow me to do this much, please."

"*Non!* I forbid you to do so. She shall do it."

"Shall she wash my feet as well?"

"Eugenie. Dare not be insolent now."

"*Pardonnez-moi,* Maman." In a meek tone, I beg to keep the boots.

"*Non!* You must give them away. How we appear is also who we are. But now, how shall you appear at court? Ah, to think that it is gone forever, that neither you nor your daughter, Eugenie, will ever wear the necklace, nor your granddaughter. It is as if you have deliberately severed our connection to the past, to our family, to France, even, and to everything we hold dear. That is what breaks my heart. And the Du Valliers! They hate us now. All that is lost, too."

"Maman, it was not my intention to sever any connections with the past. I wished only to prevent more suffering. Can you not forgive me?"

"*Non.* I am incapable of forgiveness now. What are those two to us? In France they would be considered the lowest of the lowly. You must forget all foolish notions, Eugenie, and then, only then, shall I be able to forgive you. Perhaps!"

To calm Maman—and to help staunch the new flow of tears—I agree that everything will be much different when King Louis-Charles arrives. He shall give this place the shape, the form, it now lacks. But I'm also thinking that he is but nine years old and in prison—if even alive! Still, I say nothing of these misgivings. "The new King, Maman, shall be our raison d'être. Our reason to be."

"*Precisement!* But even the Queen, the memory of our Marie Antoinette, should do that. Surely you can see this. You are an intelligent young woman, though you have acted most stupidly."

"I do see it, Maman," I say to placate her. And then all is nearly calm between us, but I ruin it by adding what Abbé La Barre told me today—that he is going to open a haber-dashery shop and will work in it himself, selling fashionable hats to all who visit here, and to other nobles who come to stay. "He is afraid that, otherwise, he may not have a certain income and will not be able to keep our chapel in good repair. It seems wise, Maman, to learn to care for oneself here. We have no servants to speak of. When the *maisons* are all built, the Americans will return to their farms. Who is going to help us make this place into something worthy of King Louis-Charles—and of the memory of our Queen? Would it not be wise to begin doing more for ourselves?" I do not add, *As Papa has advised.*

"When these Americans leave, there will always be others from the settlements around here."

"But our gold—will it last so long? Father has been learning the craft of joinery, and that is why I—"

"You are not, nor will you ever be, a maid of the kitchens."

"*Oui,* Maman."

"Here she is now. Give her those boots to take away. I forbid you to speak to her except to give an order."

"But, Maman, she is my—"

Then in front of Hannah Maman says, "Are you about

to say that she is your friend? That cannot be. Amelia is your friend. This one is nothing to you. Amelia is coming this afternoon with sheet music. Learn it, please. Use your time well. Now come, my daughter. Assure me that you shall change for the better."

She opens her arms and I go to her.

"You must be understanding," Papa tells me as we walk with Sylvette after dinner. "She is not herself these days."

None of us are!

"Papa, do you think we will ever be able to live the way we once did?"

"I do not know."

"Will you go on being a joiner if King Louis-Charles comes here?"

"*Non.* It would make your Maman too unhappy. In fact, I have all but stopped."

"You shall not be happy, will you, merely playing *boules* or cards."

"There is so much to miss, it is all blended together in a cassoulet, so I suppose another ingredient will not matter so much." He smiles to cheer me.

So much to miss. The wretchedness returns, pain everywhere piling up, stone upon stone upon stone: the boots, the necklace, and John, too. And I not being able to make bread ever again, or do anything of importance. But then I remember how I prevented a duel, and that, at least, was something of importance.

"Papa, I am weary."

"I, too."

"I simply wished to do some good."

"Be assured that you did."

"But at what cost!"

"That is sometimes the way of it."

"Papa? What if—ah, I cannot bear to even say it!"

"What is it, *chérie?* Tell me."

"I fear that Louis-Charles is dead, too. And that we may never be able to return to France. What, then, Papa?"

"Then, *chérie,* we must find our own way. The paths here are not so clearly laid out, except, perhaps, for the vicomte's few avenues. But this does not mean all is impossible, in America."

"Papa, who will we *be* here? I am not even certain who I am at this moment."

"Well, let me see. You are Eugenie Annette Marie de La Roque, and I remain Philippe August Pierre de La Roque, chevalier, comte de Saint-Simon."

His arm around me, Papa lets me cry, there in the dusk.

I finally stop, more out of exhaustion than anything else, and then call Sylvette. I want, now, my bed. And sleep. And no dreams.

But Sylvette is gone. She was here just moments ago, her white shape careening about in the near-dark. "Something has happened to her, Papa!"

"Oh, she will return to us later tonight."

"But she has never left us before!"

"She will find her way, Eugenie. As we will, in time. Come, it is getting cold, and your Maman will worry."

I call Sylvette several times, and then we turn from the wall of dark forest to a somber view of our few *maisons* and chapel. The *maisons* are dark, and the chapel, all the unglazed windows covered with pieces of velvet, brocade, or tapestry. Except for the chimney smoke, it looks like an abandoned, soulless place.

My sense of loss grows to encompass everything—our château and lands, Versailles, our Queen, our country, and now even Sylvette. *Mon Dieu, let it not be. I will do anything. I will accept all Maman's rules without question. Just let Sylvette return, s'il vous plaît. I do not think I can live, otherwise.*

Again I call her, but she does not appear. Papa steadies me as we return.

I cannot sleep. Several times I get up, thinking, *Sylvette!* Whining at the door! Jumping against it! But no. Each time it is but the wind. I imagine an owl, talons extended, plunging down upon her and carrying her away. The image is a torment until I imagine wolves chasing her. Five of them. Eight. She tires and crouches . . .

At the door I throw on my cloak and put on my mud-crusted *souliers.* I open the door and call her name.

"Eugenie!" Maman says. "You must not go out. Close the door!"

I lie down again and listen.

Hours later comes a soft tapping of our stone knocker. Quietly I rise and unbar the door.

Estelle! With Sylvette in her arms. The girl curtsies and presents wriggling Sylvette to me.

"Where did you find her?" I whisper, tears forming.

"At the river, my lady. Drinking."

Embracing the girl, I again whisper, *"Merci, merci,* Estelle." I look behind me, but the room is quiet. "You must have some reward. What do you wish? If I can grant it, then I shall."

"You are so good, my lady, but I do not wish a reward. It

is enough that Sylvette is home and that I have been able to do something for you, now."

Home.

She curtsies and then leaves in the flat light of dawn. She is wearing the velvet cloak I gave her for her escape. Her step is almost . . . regal.

The night's fire has all but died. Quickly I place two smaller logs on the embers, a traitorous act I cannot resist in my euphoria. Sylvette settles into her place on the feather bed, and I alongside her, one hand on her head while she sleeps. *Ah, Sylvette, you disobedient creature. How dare you leave me.*

On the hearth the logs catch, and soon our *maison* warms. I do not want sleep now. I want to lie here, in this quiet, and just *be* in it. With Sylvette.

Soon an idea floats clear, rising like a bubble from the froth of this small happiness.

Hannah

I look about our cabin. The floors are clean. Eight loaves of bread wait on the table. A plate of shriveled apples. Another of dried fish. And still another of raisins and walnuts. What we do not eat tonight, we will take for our journey home tomorrow.

Home. A thought bringing joy wreathed around with pain.

Father and John are finishing work on the last cabin they will build here. Father wants to be certain that the chimney is completed well.

I look at the loaves before me. The fragrance of baking still fills our cabin. No, not ours anymore.

After a while, I take one of the loaves and walk out into the day.

A spring wind eddies about, carrying bits and clumps of poplar fluff that float in the air like snow. At the Aversille cabin, I raise the river stone and let it fall against the door. Some time later it opens, and Madame d'Aversille peers out into the strong light. "For you," I tell her in French. When she takes the loaf with her trembly, crooked hand, I turn to go. But her other hand grasps my arm and draws me into the cabin. How strong she still is!

Inside, she puts the bread on her table and then turns to regard me, as I do her. All the wrinkles. The wig that is mashed down on one side, so I know that she has been having a nap. *"Au revoir,"* I tell her. Still she says naught.

But then she draws me to her. Her wig tickles my chin. I will always remember this wig! A little possum, with its tail. When she steps away again, I see that the wrinkles all about her eyes are like streamlets filled to the brim.

I tell her in French not to be sad. I am going home, to my mama and sisters and brother. Soon there will be many French people here to cheer her. And soon it will be warm, with much sun. She may even have a boat ride on the river.

Madame keeps shaking her head. The little streamlets flow, causing my own eyes to brim.

I tell her she can come visit our farm. This, I cannot imagine. Madame d'Aversille at our farm—if Mr. Coffey does not raise the rent beyond what we can pay him. This, a worry. I tell madame that my mama cooks very well, and madame will enjoy the food.

Then madame begins speaking in French I cannot understand. She goes too fast. She gestures and exclaims, and I can only watch her. While she talks, she keeps pulling at her hand, her fingers.

I back away. The open door is behind me.

Madame grasps my left hand and places something there. Then she fairly pushes me outside. With a bang the door closes.

I open my hand and see what it is.

"Non, madame, s'il vous plaît!" I call. *"C'est non necessaire!"*

I think of leaving the ring at the doorstep, but the door opens a bit—as if she sensed this thought.

"Allez, allez!" she says, shooing me away. But she places two fingers to her lips and turns her palm toward me.

Before leaving, I do the same.

The ring's stone, in the sunlight, is the red of a cardinal.

I turn back to look at the cabin I shall probably never see again. Madame is standing in the doorway.

I curtsy. "*Merci*, madame. *Merci!*"

Eugenie ☙

The chapel is again filled for yet another Requiem Mass for our late Queen. Even a few workers are present, standing outside the open doors. Apart from them—and Abbé La Barre in his black vestments—none of us wears black. None of us apparently thought to bring mourning clothes to America, which bespeaks of some blind optimism, if not our haste. A stranger looking in might think the same thing, observing us in our brilliant finery. The protocol all wrong! *L'etiquette* lacking!

Ah! But what does it matter, such an insignificant thing as cloth?

Candle flames on the altar sway in the breeze from open windows. Looking out, I see the river in the near distance. No boat passes. There is just the silvered water, its wavelets catching light and carrying it southward. And beyond the water, leafing trees, their gold-green reminding me of ancient stained glass.

We heave ourselves up with effort. We sit heavily. We whisper our responses without the least sign of vigor or conviction. Abbé La Barre's Latin may as well be Russian. It is merely sound. The Mass's solemnity, though, and the priest's slow movements do feel exactly right. I make up my own small prayer. *May you be with the angels, my Queen. May all your transgressions have been forgiven.*

After the Gospel, while others are seated and awaiting the homily, I glance at Papa and he at me. Then I rise and walk to the pulpit while Abbé La Barre seats himself at the opposite side of the sanctuary.

The murmuring sounds like waves, and then it seems as if these waves are washing right over me. I draw in breath and release it slowly. My heart pounds so, I fear Maman may hear it. She is sitting there stiffly but not looking at me at all. She seems about to weep again. Oh, Maman.

"Thank you, Abbé La Barre," I begin, "for allowing me to speak." My voice is so small! I must make it larger. I suddenly know what Hannah must have felt, trying to address us at the *fête.*

"I wish to offer apology for any distress I may have caused you these past days." I look directly at Florentine, who gazes at his knees. Maman's face is a mask. Nearby are the marquis and vicomte. I cannot look at them.

"Coming here, we had so much . . ." I look to Papa. He nods a little. *Go on, keep going.* ". . . hope. But we did not want change. Is this not true? And yet everything changes."

This is not a good beginning. The words I prepared were so much better. Now I cannot remember them.

"When we heard of our Queen's death, our hearts were wounded. We are a wounded people now. There is nothing to be done, you may think, but suffer this terrible pain that fills us completely. Perhaps, you may think, we can erect a monument here to our late King, Louis XVI, and our dear Queen, Marie Antionette. A monument of stone.

"But is not stone cold? Is it not lifeless?

"I have been thinking that *to live* may be a greater

monument. But to live how? Exactly as before?" Again I look at Maman and Papa. Again Papa nods slightly. Maman seems far away.

"We cannot, I fear. But we can live *well*. Oh, I do not mean sumptuously, as before. I mean with heart." A few words from last night's preparation finally do come to me. "A queen dies; slaves are reborn into a new life of freedom. A queen has a heart capable of sorrow and longing, but so has a slave. In the pain of grief we are all equal. So . . ." But again, all is blank. I can only look out at everyone. Aunt Sophie and Amelia and Uncle Chemin. The Aversilles. The Du Valliers. The Sevignys. Maman. Papa. Everyone is so very quiet!

"*Mes amis*, Hannah Kimbrell is a good person. She lives with heart because she considers others. It is true she is not of noble blood, but she lives . . . nobly. Even, one could say, in the very tradition of the old chivalric code. Yet we have wronged her and her family. In some respects I know why, but I do not fully understand why. Can anyone here tell me?"

I fear that Florentine will jump up to do verbal battle. Or the Du Valliers. Or even the vicomte. Yet all remain seated—and silent. Florentine's eyes meet mine briefly before he lowers them again. Madame d'Aversille slowly stands. Leaning on her stick, she says, "It is because we have been stupid. I defy anyone to say otherwise." Slowly, she sits. Her husband takes her hand.

The silence deepens. Never before have I been aware of such a silence. A vast lake of silence.

"Let us live well," I am finally able to conclude. "As a memorial to . . . our Queen."

I do not know how I find my way back to my place

alongside Papa, but somehow I do, and the Liturgy continues in its ancient, soothing rhythms, carrying us from Credo, to Sanctus, to Consecration and Communion. Someone plays the lovely hymn "Jesu, Joy of Man's Desiring" on the harpsichord, and then we sit awhile in silence before leaving the chapel. Coming into the brilliant sunlight is like waking from sleep. Could it be I have said all those artless words? Some nobles smile at me, but others look away, so I must have. The Du Valliers do not linger to speak with us. Poor Maman.

There is to be a dinner for us at *La Grande Maison,* and some nobles walk in that direction. Among them are Amelia and her family. I turn to look at the river again. Three longboats are moored at the landing. The sight of them shakes me for a moment—*the Queen!*—but that thought soon dissolves.

And there is the Kimbrell family, their barrels on a handcart, their animals—the cow, two goats, and two sheep—following behind. I recall how I fed these animals last winter. And milked Violette.

I wipe my face with both hands, smearing, I know, my powder. Maman whispers that I must collect myself. She places an arm around me and draws me closer to her, which causes the burn of fresh tears.

"Look, Maman, Alain is taking Violette, the cow. And Estelle, the goats."

Estelle leads all three animals to the side, while Alain helps the Kimbrells load their belongings. Then Monsieur Kimbrell takes a crate of chickens from the cart and carries it to Estelle. Hannah looks down at the two sheep, pats each of them, and leads them to Estelle as well. The sheep bleat. Estelle shakes her head several times, but Hannah persists as only Hannah can, and then she quickly embraces Estelle before walking toward the boats.

"Maman, they are giving their animals away!"

Maman seems to be studying the scene, her eyes still. At her mouth, the top of her closed fan. I want to run down to the landing but dare not. Yet I cannot stop more words from rushing forth. "Forgive the Kimbrells, I beg you. Intercede with the vicomte. Hannah saved you. Truly, she did. She saved you for us, Maman, and now you will have a child—our family shall! But what will she have, after so much effort?"

The Kimbrell family boards one of the boats, and rivermen shove it farther into the river. Maman looks over at Papa. I lower my head and turn away. I do not want to have that picture inside me, too, the longboat carried away on the current, and Hannah perhaps raising her arm in farewell as the sheep bleat and Violette moans.

But then Papa calls out "Stop!" in a voice far more commanding than I have ever heard it.

I open my eyes. Four rivermen lean against their poles, holding the boat still. Water piles up at its stern, creating a bunch of lace there.

Maman removes a glove and touches my cheek. Her soft hand wipes tears from each eye. "Eugenie," she whispers. "Please do not cry. It will ruin your beauty." But her own eyes shine with tears, and at that moment she is most beautiful. Then Papa is gesturing for the longboat to return to the landing. Again Maman leans to me. "He is quite eccentric, no? What a spectacle he again creates! No doubt we shall never hear the end of it."

But she is smiling somewhat. With all my strength I embrace her and hang on while the Kimbrells disembark and walk up the landing toward us, their expressions as fearful as ours must have been so many months ago.

Together, Maman, Papa, and I go to meet them.

When we are quite close, I step forward and take Hannah's hand in my own gloved one. It is like gripping a tree limb. I see her surprise, even shock, but then fear leaves her eyes, and she is again the serene Hannah I know.

And have come—I see this now—to love.

Epilogue

1794

Septembre / September

৫৬ Hannah

The baby—Marie—looks like a fat little queen in a white gown with a wide lace collar. For her crown, a puffy, lace-edged cap. Eugenie carries her to her cradle, and we take turns rocking it while Eugenie sings the first verse of "Over in the Meadow" in French and then I in English. Soon the baby falls asleep smiling. But we go on rocking her cradle—and watching her. She is so sweet. So perfect. Now there is just the gentle thumping of the cradle moving back and forth over floorboards. 'Tis very like slow heartbeat. I give thanks for Eugenie and for this new little one. I pray that she and her family will find here, in our new country, all that is good. It is much to ask, I know, but let it be, *s'il vous plaît!*

In a wonderful whirl of thought, I imagine Eugenie wearing a necklace of river stones, round and polished and holding within themselves water, light, and time, so much time. And the stones linked with silver, just as the river has linked us all together. Surely if Father can make such fine boots, John and I can fashion such a thing.

We shall learn.

Eugenie ꙮ

We travel downriver some distance farther than Sylvette and I traveled last spring—or was it winter?—on our little floats of ice. This time our boat, poled by Mr. Kimbrell, John, and Papa, lands at a small settlement, and Monsieur Kimbrell arranges for a wagon with seats in its bed to convey us somewhere. Seeing that wagon, I shudder, but holding Sylvette, I climb in and sit alongside Maman and Papa. Little Marie has been looking about in wonder. The river today is a glorious amber color, with great green trees on either side. For Marie, all this will be something as natural as our château, with its fields and meadows, was for us. Something even of solace, perhaps. ·

A short distance beyond the settlement, the wagon comes to a stop on a rise, quite high, above the Susquehanna. The others jump down nimbly. Maman and I take much longer to gather our gowns about ourselves and, aided by Papa, carefully climb down. And of course I have Sylvette and Maman has little Marie. Monsieur Kimbrell leads the way to several enormous flat rocks stuck into the cliff like tabletops.

"Prayer rocks, they're called," Monsieur Kimbrell tells us. He explains that American Indians once came here to give thanks for rain or a good harvest or to offer prayers of supplication. I keep tight hold of Sylvette's leash as we stand on one of the flat rocks and look to the west, the south, and the east. In each direction, a seemingly endless landscape of forested mountains undulates to the pale blue of horizon and dissolves there in mist.

Mon Dieu, such a vast land, this America. It is where we shall remain, Papa and Maman have decided. Maman does not wish to risk Marie's life in France, or mine. *Perhaps, Eugenie, when you are both much older, you shall return—if it is safe. Meanwhile, we will create what we must, here.*

Even my bones seemed to tremble when I heard those words. I knew not whether with joy or sadness.

And I have made a decision as well. I shall paint! Papa and Maman responded with one word. *"Magnifique!"* Then they embraced me with what might have been an American bear's strength.

None of this could we have imagined last autumn, down there in our wet boats, in the mist and fog.

"Look, Eugenie," Hannah whispers. She points to a plain bounded by a horseshoe curve in the river. "Azilum."

So charming, really, viewed from this height. So pastoral and lovely. The tiny *maisons* and grazing animals. The rows of fruit trees and vines. The vegetable gardens and flower gardens. I close my eyes and thank Our Lady and then look once more at the river, today a wondrous vein of light.

"Come," Papa says. "Our *pique-nique* awaits!"

"One moment, please!" I beg. Quickly I find my sketch book and pencil while Hannah keeps hold of Sylvette's leash.

It will be my first painting. *Azilum.* Everything I am seems to flow down to my hand, and then there is the Susquehanna, curving as if protectively around the clearing with its tiny structures and smaller animals and trees. Then forest and distant ridges, and clouds. There must also be light!

I must learn how to create a mantle of light gilding trees and river and houses and animals and boats. Everything.

When I close my sketchbook, my fingers seem to flutter with life. Perhaps angels have taken up residence there.

In the shade of a great tree, Hannah and I open baskets and set out bread, newly churned butter, tomatoes, cucumbers, and savory smoked fish. And, too, a small wheel of Estelle and Alain's Camembert cheese. We place everything upon the braided rug Hannah has made especially for today and which she is giving us for the new room in our *petite maison*. Even the Queen herself might have treasured this rug, in its autumn forest hues.

Soon Hannah, John, and Mr. Kimbrell will return to their farm. I cannot bear to think of this, yet know they cannot remain here indefinitely. There is so much work on their farm now, Hannah says, for it is harvest time. *Their* farm—Papa has seen to this. But they are to come back here next summer. Until then, another winter! We will manage. We are no longer the same helpless creatures we were last autumn. And I need all that time, for I want Hannah and John to be proud of me when I show them my drawings and paintings. Hannah does not know this yet, but *Azilum* will be hers.

I meet Maman's eyes as I begin slicing one of my loaves on a cutting board of smooth wood. She fears a mishap, but I slice with care and then lean back. The aroma alone is enough to bring tears.

Together we give thanks in French and in English and begin our feast.

Author's Note

Waiting for the Queen was inspired by its setting—now a state historical park in northeastern Pennsylvania. Even today the place is remote, windswept, and surrounded by forest. In 1793 it must have looked like some forbidding place of exile to those members of the court of Versailles and other nobles who sought sanctuary there after fleeing the terrors of the French Revolution. I wondered what the nobles might have felt, having lost so much and then journeying so far only to find a frontier wilderness of half-built cabins and looming forest. Accustomed as they were to silk and damask and servants, but now having to make do with cramped dwellings, plain wooden chairs, and little if any help, how would these nobles react? Would they give way to grief and despair or become stronger as a result? And what about when they learn of the Queen's execution by the guillotine? How hard might that be for them?

These were some of the thoughts and questions that arose in a rush of emotion as I walked about the site one somber November afternoon, a cold northwest wind sweeping across the Susquehanna River. I was the only visitor that day, and the solitude heightened all of my thoughts. I could almost see the nobles there in their finery, wondering where on earth they were. At that moment, *Waiting for the Queen* began taking shape in my imagination. As it did, I was inspired, too, by the way the word *Azilum* merges both French and English (*asile* + asylum) just as the geography and experience of the settlers blended French and American cultures into something altogether new.

Two of the novel's characters are historical personages: the Vicomte de Noailles and the Marquis Antoine Omer Talon. And several characters alluded to are historical figures: Marie Antoinette, of course; her husband, King Louis XVI; their daughter Marie-Thérèse; and their son Louis-Charles, the titular king upon his father's death in January of 1793. Louis-Charles died, it's believed, two years after his mother's death.

In the late 1780s and 1790s, the French nobility was regarded far more sympathetically in America than in France. There, during the French Revolution, nobles were scorned, hunted as traitors, tried as criminals, and very often executed. America had no such animosities toward the French aristocrats but generally regarded them with favor and sympathy. The young Marquis de Lafayette, for example, was a popular hero of the American Revolution. He served as a major-general under General George Washington and became Washington's personal friend. Serving under Lafayette was Louis-Marie, Vicomte de Noailles, who in France, ironically, had worked toward abolishing aristocratic privileges.

So when the Vicomte de Noailles, along with the Marquis Antoine Omer Talon, hoped to purchase land in America so that fleeing French aristocrats might find sanctuary and found a settlement, they encountered not resistance but a great deal of enthusiastic support, particularly from two Pennsylvanians, Senator Robert Morris, financier, merchant, and land speculator, and John Nicholson, then comptroller-general of Pennsylvania.

Senator Morris owned lands in the north-central wilderness of Pennsylvania and knew of an area—a meadowland of about sixteen hundred acres formed by a horseshoe bend in the Susquehanna River—that might be a good place for the aristocrats' settlement. Titles to the land had to be purchased from nearby settlers and laborers had to be hired' for building cabins for the first émigrés, who arrived in the autumn of 1793.

By 1798, some were calling the place Frenchtown, but it was also coming to be known as French Azilum or, simply, Azilum. It was a prosperous settlement. Its log houses had porches and well-built chimneys, shutters, window glass, and, inside, fine wallpaper. The village had its own chapel, dairy, gristmill, blacksmith's shop, and distillery. Surrounding the 413 house plots along a gridiron pattern of avenues were farm plots, orchards, vineyards, and pastures. Settlers even produced potash and pearlash, which could be bartered for other goods. Potash and pearlash were used in making fertilizer, soap, glass, and gunpowder.

Eventually, there were a number of shops, a school-house, a theater, and at least two inns. Famous people came to visit this "French Arcadia." Among them were Charles Maurice de Talleyrand, a French statesman and later advisor and confidant of Napoléon Bonaparte. The hugely popular Marquis de Lafayette also visited. Louis Philippe, Duc de Orleans and a future king of France, was another such grand visitor.

But *Waiting for the Queen* takes place before all of this

success—in fact, it takes place right at the beginning, when all is new and raw and unsettled and, for those first émigrés, quite daunting.

Napoléon Bonaparte eventually granted amnesty to the French émigrés, and many returned to France in the first decade of the nineteenth century. Some chose, however, to move to coastal cities in the southern United States, such as Charleston, Savannah, and New Orleans. Others returned to Santo Domingo in the Caribbean. Most, finally, did not adapt to frontier life or choose to mingle with their new American neighbors. By the time of French amnesty toward the aristocrats, there was some hostility toward the French settlers because France, now at war with England, had begun seizing American ships. America wanted to remain neutral, and this angered France. Despite this animosity, a number of émigrés chose to stay in America, and a few even remained in the beautiful hill country surrounding the plain in the bend of the Susquehanna River.

It's common belief, tinged with local folklore, that Marie Antoinette and her two surviving children (two others had died before the French Revolution) intended to seek sanctuary at Azilum. No document has yet surfaced to support this belief, though recent archaeological excavations at the site do appear to indicate that, in addition to the smaller structures, a "grand house" had been built at the settlement. What is historically accepted, though, is that there were plans to free Marie Antoinette and her children from prison and get them out of France. And, too, news of her execution did take months to reach the settlement. More may be learned in years to come.

Meanwhile, we have imagination.

Bibliography

Although *Waiting for the Queen* is a work of fiction, I tried to be as historically accurate as possible in setting the story. To this end, I consulted the French Azilum material on file at the Bradford County Historical Society and Museum in Towanda, Pennsylvania, namely the following:

"The Fascinating Story of Historic French Asylum (or Azilum) in Pennsylvania, 1793–1800." Address by the Honorable A. C. Fanning at the dedication of the monument at Frenchtown, Pennsylvania, June 14, 1916, in memory of the French Royalist refugees. Reprinted from the Towanda *Daily Review.* Rock Mount, 2nd Edition, March 1932.

Hagerman, Alice. "The Village of French Azilum," *The Settler, A Quarterly Magazine of History and Biography.* Bradford County Historical Society, Towanda, Pennsylvania. February 1955.

Murray, Elsie. *Azilum: French Refugee Village on the Susquehanna.* (A booklet.) Tioga Point Museum: Athens, Pennsylvania, 1956.

Murray, Elsie. "French Experiments in Pioneering in Northern Pennsylvania." (Offprint.) *The Pennsylvania Magazine of History and Biography,* April 1944.

"French Azilum," (a leaflet). Pennsylvania Historical and
Museum Commission, Division of History, Harrisburg,
Pennsylvania.

In addition, I read through numerous newspaper clippings,
several leaflets about the site, and looked at maps as well as
lists of refugees.
Other helpful sources include:

Bartlett, John Russell. *Dictionary of Americanisms.* John Wiley
& Sons, Inc.: Hoboken, New Jersey and Canada, 2003.

Bradfield, Nancy. *Costumes in Detail, Women's Dress,
1730–1930.* Plays Inc.: Boston, 1968, 1975.

Fradin, Dennis B. *The Pennsylvania Colony.* Childrens Press:
Chicago, 1988.

Gorsline, Douglas. *What People Wore: A Visual History
of Dress from Ancient Times to 20th Century America.*
Bonanza Books: New York, MCMLI, MCMLII.

Kennedy, Pamela. *A Christmas Celebration: Traditions and
Customs from Around the World.* Ideals Childrens Books:
Nashville, Tennessee, 1992.

Philip, Neil, Ed. *Singing America.* Viking: New York, 1995.

Rockwell, Anne. *Savez-vous Planter les Choux and Other
French Songs.* The World Publishing Company:
Cleveland and New York, 1969.

Seymour, John. *The Forgotten Crafts.* Alfred A. Knopf: New
York, 1984.

For general information about Maria Antoinette and the French Revolution as well as Quakerism, I consulted the 1957 edition of *Encyclopedia Britannica*.

Finally, another helpful source for an understanding of the French Revolution:

The French Revolution by the editors of *Horizon Magazine*, in consultation with Professor David L. Dowd. American Heritage Publishing, Inc.: New York, 1963.

Works of fiction useful for an understanding of the background:

Anderson, Laurie Halse. *Fever—1793*. Alladin Paperbacks: New York, London, Toronto, Sydney, Singapore, 2002.

Erickson, Carolly. *The Hidden Diary of Marie Antoinette*. St. Martin's Press: New York, 2005.

I'm most grateful to Denise Golden of the Bradford County Historical Society and Museum in Towanda, Pennsylvania, for making available a wealth of material concerning French Azilum. Kathy Kretzmer, Bonnie House, and Linda Green, librarians at the Vestal Public Library, in Vestal, New York, helped in all the ways good librarians are noted for—with their expertise, their interest over the years, and their invariable good will and cheer. To Kathleen Kirk, a longtime dear friend, my great thanks for reading early drafts of this novel and for patiently answering numerous questions regarding the French language. I'm also deeply grateful to Ben Barnhart, my first editor, for his enthusiasm, keen editorial skill, and valuable comments and suggestions. In addition, Allison Wigen, Associate Editor, and the wonderful staff at Milkweed Editions deserve praise and thanks for the care taken with the manuscript of this novel. And finally, to my husband and first reader, Jerry, my boundless gratitude for his sustaining presence in this writer's life and in the life of our family.

From an early age Joanna Higgins loved books and writing. Born and raised in northern Michigan, she developed a taste for the fiction of Jack London and John Steinbeck and later earned degrees in English from the University of Michigan (MA) and Binghamton University (PhD). She studied writing with John Gardner and has also taught at colleges and universities. She now lives with her family in upstate New York and northeastern Pennysylvania.

Higgins is the author of three books for adults—*The Importance of High Places*, *A Soldier's Book*, and *Dead Center*. *Waiting for the Queen* is her first novel for young readers.

Interior design by Connie Kuhnz
Typeset in Adobe Caslon Pro
by BookMobile Design and Publishing Services